Harlequin Romances

OTHER

Harlequin Romances

by ISOBEL CHACE

THE CLOUDED VEIL

by

ISOBEL CHACE

Harlequin Books

TORONTO • LONDON • NEW YORK • AMSTERDAM • SYDNEY • WINNIPEG

Original hardcover edition published in 1976
by Mills & Boon Limited

ISBN 0-373-02023-6

Harlequin edition published November 1976
Second printing March 1977
Third Printing April 1977

Printed in Canada

CHAPTER ONE

IT was not the first time that Elinor had been to Morocco. She stood in the airport lounge and considered her fellow travellers, wondering what was taking each one of them away from England's shores. Most were probably on holiday, but there was a sprinkling of those who had evidently seen the sun often and for a long space of time, as their faces could bear witness. They were not all of them Moors, but they all had that ease of bearing and sureness of movement that the constant wearing of summer clothes seems to bring.

'Mrs. Wild?'

Elinor turned quickly and met the smile of the uniformed man beside her with a small jolt of surprise.

'Y-yes?' she admitted hesitantly. There was something familiar about him, but she couldn't remember what.

'You don't remember me,' the young man accused her. 'I thought a bride always remembered every moment of *the* day!'

Elinor smiled wanly.

'You were a friend of Zachary's,' she said expressionlessly.

'That's right! I came over to say how sorry I am.'

Elinor nodded. There had been so many people offering sympathy and asking if there was anything that they could do. But none of them could do a thing. She had had to get used to her widowed estate alone, away from her father, and away from the friends she had known in childhood.

'It seems a very long time since that day,' she said quietly.

'Does it?' He smiled sympathetically. 'But you've been

away, haven't you? You haven't been riding on our aeroplanes?'

That was what his uniform was, she concluded with relief. She had been thinking that she should have known more about him, but she had been unable to remember the first thing about him. When Zachary had been there she had never really noticed anyone else.

'What have you been doing since——?' the young man inquired, not knowing how to complete his inquiry.

'I came to England, to nurse. I've just got my S.R.N. and now I'm going home.'

'Ah yes,' he said. 'I seem to remember that that was what you wanted to do. I suppose getting married changed your plans for a while?'

Elinor winced. 'Well, yes,' she said.

'I say,' he said humbly, 'did I say something? I only meant——'

'Yes, I know. You're being very kind. It's only that I shall have to get used to it all over again! Hardly anyone in England knew, and that made it easier to forget, in a way.'

'Then you haven't really managed to forget all about him?' the young man asked bluntly.

Elinor brushed the tears out of her eyes and laughed.

'Of course I have!' she said bravely. 'It was all so very long ago, wasn't it?'

She had not seen Morocco for the last two years. The last time she had made the journey by the cheapest possible method. She had been on holiday, returning home to visit her father after the first year of her training. It had all been a tremendous adventure, taking the train through France and Spain and then crossing the Straits of Gibraltar on the Spanish ferry that left daily from Algeciras.

It was on the ferry that she had met Zachary Wild.

'Well, well, well,' he had said as he had tucked her into a deck-chair beside him. 'Fancy meeting you here!'

6

She had been doubtful of his attentions right from the beginning, but now she was more worried still because she was quite sure she had never met him before.

'Have we met?' she had asked him.

'Of course we've met!' he had retorted. 'Do you think I make conversation with total strangers?'

'I don't know,' she had answered, incurably honest.

His eyes had danced.

'I really think you don't believe me!' he had teased her. Elinor had bitten her lip and had said nothing at all, because, after all, it was difficult to accuse anyone as dashing as this of being an out-and-out liar. 'Why don't you believe me?' he had insisted. 'Don't I look like a perfectly respectable young man?'

'I don't know,' she had said again. It was something about which she was not prepared to make up her mind. He had a slight accent that flattened his vowels into a faint drawl that was ugly but was not unattractive. It was not an accent that she could place and it added to the sense of mystery that surrounded him.

'I shall have to think of some clever way to persuade you that I'm quite harmless,' he had said, completely confident that he could overcome any scruples, reasonable or not. 'Shall we go and have lunch?'

She had nodded. Nothing like Zachary Wild had ever come her way before and she could hardly believe her own good fortune. The wine he had ordered at the meal had loosened her tongue and she had been warmed by his obvious interest and his laughing asides.

It had not been quite so easy to introduce him to her father. Walter Kendon had elected to live in Morocco soon after the death of his wife, when Elinor had still been a child. Nobody had ever known why he should have done such a thing. He was everything that one would imagine a staid, suburban businessman to be. He seldom took risks and he liked his life to fall into accustomed patterns with

7

himself in the centre of events. He distrusted foreigners and was only really at home with other men of his own kind. And yet he had come to Morocco and had started a business there and had made a great deal of money, but he was still a foreigner living in a foreign land. After all these years, he was still the only man Elinor knew of in Morocco who still wore a dark suit, complete with waistcoat, no matter how hot it was or what he was doing.

'I've told you before not to speak to strangers out here,' he greeted his daughter bleakly.

Elinor had kissed him warmly on the cheek, disregarding his lack of response. 'Zachary says he's not a stranger,' she replied calmly.

Walter Kendon had looked at the young man with dispassionate interest. 'Indeed?'

Zachary had held out his hand. 'I'm Dr. Wild, sir——'

Mr. Kendon had pursed up his mouth with disapproval. 'I think I've heard of Dr. Wild,' he had said, and it had not sounded like a compliment. 'Where are you off to next?'

Zachary Wild had grinned at the older man, his accent more pronounced than ever.

'I shall be around,' he had drawled.

Elinor had been shattered at having to part from him even for quite a short time.

'You will come to Meknes,' she had urged him. 'I shall be waiting for you!'

'I'll come,' he had said.

Her father had been visibly displeased. 'What are that young man's intentions?' he had asked Elinor as they had driven the miles to his home in Meknes. 'Marriage?'

Elinor had grinned cheekily at him, 'Oh, I do hope so!' she had exclaimed.

'Shamelessness!' her father had snorted. 'Why, you don't know the first thing about him!'

'But you do!' she had answered confidently.

'A most unsteady young man!' he had said with disap-

8

proval. 'To begin with, he's an Australian. Could have had a decent, safe practice in Sydney——'

'Oh, is he a doctor?' Elinor had interrupted him.

Her father had frowned and had gone on exactly where he had left off.

'Or even in London. Nothing to stop him! But he has to come to Morocco to treat the Rif, the Berbers, Arabs, even the blue men from the south! I don't suppose any of them pay him a penny! He's even learned all their dialects and eats their food. Wonder he hasn't been poisoned by now!'

'But what a fine thing to do!' Elinor had exclaimed.

'It's dangerous and irresponsible!' her father had snubbed her. 'What future has he got?'

Elinor hadn't bothered to answer. She was too full of dreams and romantic excitement to care.

The young man who had been to her wedding glanced down at his watch.

'It's time I was going,' he announced. 'I'm flying you out this trip. I hope the knowledge won't make you nervous!'

Elinor laughed and shook her head.

'I'm sure I couldn't be in safer hands,' she answered.

The young man still hesitated.

'I liked Zachary very much,' he said awkwardly. 'I'm glad you are taking it so well.'

Elinor nodded coolly.

'I've had time,' she reminded him. 'Time disposes of everything.'

'I suppose so,' he stammered, and went out through a door marked 'Private' to get the aeroplane ready for the flight.

A few minutes later Elinor took her seat in the aeroplane herself and automatically fastened her safety belt. It was only a matter of hours now and she would be home. Home in that incredibly beautiful house where her father lived, that had once been part of the palace of one of Moulay

9

Ismail's sons, in the days when that king had looked across at Louis XIV's Palace of Versailles and had decided to build a palace for himself on the same grand scale. Mr. Kendon's present house stretched around a courtyard, so designed that it was always full of sunshine, and the walls and ceilings were so elaborately and intricately carved that Elinor had long ago given up counting the different geometric designs that decorated every corner in the best Moroccan tradition.

Yes, she would be home, but there would be no Zachary to greet her. Instead there would be her father's new partner, Gerard Roche, who she knew to be nice but suspected was also rather dull. Oh well, she thought, it didn't really matter. Zachary had been every girl's adolescent dream, but sooner or later we all of us have to grow up.

Zachary had been as good as his word. She had never known when he would come or where she could expect to find him, but she saw him often and she loved him more and more.

He had even teased her about her choice of career.

'What good will being a nurse do you?' he had asked her. 'Your father will never let you work out here.'

She had smiled slowly. 'Perhaps it won't depend on my father!' she had answered.

Zachary had pretended to look puzzled. 'Now what sparkling idea have you got into your head?' he had asked. 'I do believe that underneath all that care for your father you've secretly been making your own plans for the future!'

'Well, what if I have?'

He had shaken his head at her.

'Now that calls for quite an answer. I shall have to think about it first.' He had waved an idle hand at her. 'I hadn't realised that you were such a forward young lady!'

Elinor had blushed. 'I didn't say anything!' she had said defensively.

'No,' he had retorted, 'but you thought it!'

She had laughed and felt suddenly brave. 'Well then?' she had pressed him.

'My love,' he had said softly, 'you don't know what you're doing. I live such a precarious life—irresponsible as your father says! Have you thought of that?'

She had nodded briefly.

'I think it's very admirable to be a doctor here,' she had said firmly. 'I wouldn't have it any other way.'

He had kissed her then and she felt as though she was drowning in his arms. Her father could say what he liked, but she couldn't have behaved any differently if she had tried. Zachary was everything to her and she was quite helpless against his warm charm that was as hot as the Moroccan sun and as romantic as any of the age-old tales she had heard of the fascinating Moor.

'When will you marry me?' he had asked her.

'As soon as it can be arranged,' she had answered quickly, and a deep satisfaction came to them both. In some way they were already tied together in spirit.

Walter Kendon had been furious when she had told him that she and Zachary were to be married.

'I won't have anything to do with it!' he had stormed at her.

'It won't make any difference,' she had warned him, equally firm and looking very like him. 'We've had fun together and I should hate to lose you, but I *can't* lose Zachary!'

In the end Mr. Kendon had given way. Elinor and Zachary had been married in the courtyard of his house with the sun dancing on the orange trees that gave such pleasant shade to them. The orange trees had been in full blossom and Elinor had thought that their rich scent would remain with her for as long as she lived. Zachary, for once in an English suit and looking completely strange and serious, had exchanged vows with her with a tenderness she

11

had not thought him capable of, and then they had all sat down to dinner, watching the sun slip from the reddened sky to be replaced by the outsize stars that burn over Africa. It had been very late before the last of the guests had departed and Mr. Kendon had grunted at them before making his own way to bed. Then there had been only she and Zachary left.

'Well, my love,' he had said softly, 'are you prepared to agree now that we must have met somewhere before?'

'I'm prepared to admit anything!' Elinor had assured him, her eyes alight with laughter. 'But I should like to know where it was that we met?'

His smile had grown more gentle and she had loved him so much that it had hurt.

'Where else but in my dreams?' he had asked her.

And he had kissed her gently on the nose.

'Will you please fasten your safety belts and extinguish your cigarettes. We are coming in to land at Tangiers airport in approximately five minutes. The local time is exactly four p.m. We hope you have had a pleasant flight and that you will enjoy your stay in Morocco.'

Elinor awoke with a bang. It could only be imagination, but she thought she could already feel the warmth of the sun and the unique smell of dust and black tobacco that lingered in the streets of Moroccan towns. Two years was a long time to have been away. Things would have changed and places that she had loved and visited with Zachary would have been torn down to make way for other, more modern buildings. Perhaps even her father would be different. She remembered him vividly as she had last seen him—saddened, but peculiarly triumphant—and she shivered. They would have to get to know one another all over again, she thought, if they were going to recapture the affection that had existed between them when she had been a child.

12

The plane came to a stop and she reached up and pulled down her small overnight bag and let her safety belt slip away from her. It would not be very long now before she actually trod on Moroccan soil. She had come home.

Her marriage to Zachary had been short and vivid. They had lived in her father's house because Zachary hadn't got a house of his own. He held a daily surgery in the house of a rich Moor who let him have a room there free of charge, but he would not allow Elinor to go with him, or to help him in any way.

'We're still on honeymoon, darling!' he had protested. 'Besides, you haven't finished your training, have you?'

So Elinor had waited impatiently for him to return from his daily task. She quite understood that he had to do it, but the loneliness of waiting for him to come back to her had been a foretaste of the long loneliness that was to come.

Daily she had fallen deeper in love with Zachary. Her father's continued disapproval scarcely registered with her at all. She was Mrs. Zachary Wild, and nothing could have given her greater happiness.

In actual fact her marriage lasted scarcely a fortnight before Zachary had disappeared. Even now Elinor could remember little of that night. She had been aware of two men coming in through their window, strangers who had been completely anonymous in their Arab clothing, with turkish towelling wound round their heads as turbans and dressed in white, so that they looked like so many ghosts prowling around the room.

'What do you want?' Zachary had asked them in Arabic.

'The doctor,' they had replied briefly.

Zachary had nodded his head and begun to dress.

'I am the doctor. What is the matter?'

There had followed a lengthy explanation that Elinor had only half heard, and anyway she couldn't understand much of what they were saying.

'Will you be long?' she had asked Zachary sleepily.

'Not a minute longer than I can help!' he had said, and had kissed her softly on the cheek. 'Don't fret, darling. I'll be back!'

But he had not come back. They had searched for him, of course. The Moroccan government had done everything they possibly could to discover where he had gone. But there had been no sign of Zachary at the end of any of the clues they had found. In the end they had come and reported the fact to Elinor, their proud faces sad and bewildered.

'We know that he went with the people of the Chleuh, of the Anti-Atlas valleys. Many of them come to the towns to work as grocers, for here they can grow rich, sending money home to their own valleys to buy land and position among their own people. But the doctor is not in the Anti-Atlas. Or, if he is, we cannot find him. We are very sorry, *madame*, but we can hold out no hope that he is alive. We think that some other tribesmen must have sent the Chleuh for him, not daring to come themselves, and that afterwards they killed him.'

Elinor had shrunk into herself in an agony of disbelief.

'Dead?' she had repeated helplessly. It really didn't seem possible as far as Zachary was concerned. He had always been so vibrantly alive.

'We are sorry, *madame*,' the officials had repeated. 'We are convinced that the doctor is no longer alive and we are closing our file on him. We are quite sure that he is dead.'

Mr. Kendon had pointed out heavily that they were very likely concealing some of the facts to spare her feelings. He himself could only be relieved that his daughter had escaped from an entanglement that he could only think of as unfortunate.

'Why don't you go back to England and finish your training?' he had suggested later when he had become worried about her increasing listlessness.

'Then no one would go on looking!' Elinor had retorted sharply.

'I would,' he had promised. But no one could bring themselves to believe any longer that there was any hope. Her father had taken Elinor's passport and had had the designation in it changed to 'widow', and that had seemed to her to be the final reality. Even she had begun to believe that Zachary was dead and that no amount of wishing was going to make it any different.

'All right,' she had said at last, ashen and exhausted. 'I shall go back to England. It will be two years before I need come back to this house anyway!'

But for months she had gone on hoping just the same. Her father exported Moroccan leather goods to Europe and was constantly meeting the different tribesmen who brought their wares to him. But none of them had ever heard of Zachary. And one day, almost unknowingly, she had finally accepted that Zachary was really and truly dead. She had not known happiness since that day, but at least the certainty was better than the endless hoping. Slowly and with a courage that she had not known she had possessed, she had begun to rebuild her life.

Elinor stumbled out of the aircraft, stretching her cramped legs after all the hours of sitting. The sun was full and golden, just as she remembered it always was in the afternoons, and she paused for an instant to really enjoy the feel of it, allowing the others to rush into the Customs before her, before she too went through the formalities of entering any country and went to find her father, sighing because she knew that she still had the long drive to Meknes before her and she was tired already.

But her father was not there. Elinor rescued her checked baggage from the porter and put it down near where the cars were coming and going, picking up and putting down passengers for the airport. The people were immediately familiar and dear to her in their variety. Many of the women were still veiled, looking like well-tailored nuns, with finely embroidered handkerchiefs stitched into place over their faces. Some others, less well off, bundled themselves into sheet-like veils which they held across their faces with one hand, leaving only a peephole through which one eye could peer out at where they were going. The men, though, showed better how Morocco had been a meeting place for all races since the beginning of history. Their faces were Grecian, Phoenician, Berber, Arab, or Negro. They met and talked to one another, like so many statues from the museums of the ancient world suddenly come to life.

At last, when Elinor had practically despaired of seeing her father, there seemed to be only one man left who had come to meet her plane. He looked lost and worried as he studied everybody around him. Elinor bit her lip to keep herself from smiling. This, she was quite sure, was Gerard Roche, exactly as she had imagined him to be. With a quick sigh she went over to him.

'Have you come from Mr. Kendon?' she asked him gently.

His immediate look of relief made her want to laugh again. The young man flushed shyly.

'You must be Elinor!' he exclaimed. 'I didn't like to barge up to you in case I was wrong. Your father has told me so much about you——' He broke off awkwardly. 'All nice things, of course! But he didn't tell me what you looked like. I was getting rather desperate.'

But Elinor wasn't listening.

'I suppose he told you all about Zachary?' she said abruptly.

'Well, yes,' he agreed. 'I say, do you mind awfully? It must have been terrible, of course, but——'

Elinor looked him straight in the eyes. 'But what?' she insisted.

Mr. Roche gulped helplessly. 'It was two years ago,

wasn't it? I mean, from what your father said—— Oh dear! He said not to mention that!'

Elinor smiled, liking him just as her father had said she would.

'My father didn't like Zachary,' she said flatly. 'I think he was rather relieved when—when it all happened. But it's all in the past now and life goes on.'

'Yes,' he agreed with a knowledgeable, man-of-the-world look. 'I'm awfully glad you feel like that because it will be jolly to have you around. Your father is awfully nice to me and all that, but he isn't very companionable, if you know what I mean?'

Elinor giggled. 'I know *exactly*!' she assured him. 'By the way, where is he?'

Gerard Roche flushed. 'He didn't come,' he explained uneasily. 'He didn't feel very well, and anyway, we thought it would be nice if I were to meet you. My name is Gerard Roche.'

Elinor shook his proffered hand. 'I thought you must be. My father wrote and told me about you.' She smiled at him. 'He told me you're French, but you speak English remarkably well!'

Gerard Roche looked pleased. 'I'm a bit of both, actually. Even my name could be either English or French. But at the moment I'm handling the French side of your father's business. It makes things easier to have a French national doing that. It's going very well,' he added on a note of pride.

'That's good! I'd like my father to retire on a note of prosperity!' Elinor congratulated him flippantly.

'But that's the whole point!' Gerard exploded. 'He won't ever retire until he's got you comfortably settled! And he ought to——' He hid his face from her as he stooped to pick up the suitcases. 'Come along, I'll show you where the car is.'

'Why should he?' Elinor asked, meekly following him,

into the hot sun.

'I-I shouldn't have said anything,' he muttered. 'Only I'm jolly glad you've come at last. He needs someone to keep an eye on him.'

'Isn't he well?' Elinor asked soberly.

'He's not as young as he was,' Gerard said cheerfully, 'and he works too hard.'

'He always did!' Elinor remembered ruefully.

Gerard helped her into the car and stowed her luggage away in the boot, carefully locking it, before he got into the car himself.

'I say, I haven't scared you, have I? Your father's quite all right, you know. It's just that he ought to ease off a bit and it isn't easy to persuade him that I can manage.'

Elinor nodded, but she said nothing. She hadn't been thinking about her father at all. She had been thinking how unbearable it was to be driving in a French car without having Zachary beside her.

'Anyway,' Gerard went on happily, 'you mustn't think that that's the only reason why I'm so glad to see you.' He looked at her shyly and, to her surprise, she could feel herself blushing at the warm regard in his eyes. 'You're much prettier than I thought you would be,' he said.

CHAPTER TWO

IT was dark when they passed through the magnificently ornate Bab El Mansour into the old part of Meknes and along the narrow streets to her father's home. A few men stood in the shadows, gossiping with their neighbours, and turned idly to see who was passing. Only the cafés blazed with light, contrasting vividly with the blackness all about them, lit only by an occasional gleam that escaped from the doorway of one of the 'secret houses, hinting at the busy, virile life that went on behind the strong windowless walls that lined the narrow streets.

Mr. Kendon had been waiting for the car and he came running out to greet them, holding his daughter close.

'I've missed you, pet,' he said with a catch in his voice. 'Has it been worth it?'

'I think so,' said Elinor. 'I'm a fully qualified nurse now!'

He hugged her again.

'What a stubborn minx you are!' he teased her. 'But it will be nice to have you to myself again. I have been looking forward to it and making plans.'

Elinor winced. 'Not too many plans!' she pleaded. 'I want to put my new skill to work now I'm back home.'

Her father looked hurt. 'You're not harking back to the past, are you? That was a nightmare that never really happened! You were lonely before, but now we have young Gerard with us and he'll help to keep you amused.'

'It will be a pleasure!' the young man said gallantly.

Elinor bit her lip. She had forgotten the awkwardnesses of living with her father. In London she had become accustomed to pleasing herself what she did. It would not be altogether easy to be the daughter of the house once again.

'I don't suppose Monsieur Roche will want to be bothered with me all the time,' she said primly. But that young man only looked the more eager.

'No, really!' he protested. 'I can't tell you how much I've been looking forward to your coming.'

Elinor could feel herself warming to him. It was very pleasant to feel his obvious admiration for her and to know herself attractive in his eyes. It was so long since any man had looked at her other than as a nurse at his bedside.

Her father looked sideways at her, half laughing at her.

'Don't look at me for help!' he said. 'You know that I should only encourage him!'

Elinor's own laughter came bubbling to the surface.

'I believe you would!' she said, and she didn't think about Zachary at all.

The house was just as she had remembered it. The subtle scent of the carved black timbers and the intricacies of the designs cut into the ceilings and walls were all still there and were just as beautiful as ever. It was like walking into paradise when they walked through the tough weather-worn wooden front door from the dark narrow street outside.

'It's so good to be home!' she breathed.

'That's how I always feel,' her father agreed. 'The height of Arab culture is in these rooms, and I must say I appreciate it. Perhaps the chairs could be more comfortable, but then I've always imported my own from England, so I get the best of both worlds!'

Elinor went through the rooms, recalling this and that scene from her childhood. She had always lived with her father ever since she could remember. Her mother had died before they had come to Morocco and Elinor couldn't now remember the house they had lived in in England. She knew that it had been small and comfortless and that her father had often wished that his spirit of adventure had led him to Africa earlier. Once in Morocco, he had mastered the national craft of working with leather and had begun to export odd pieces to Europe. The business had flourished and Walter Kendon was now at home in his adopted land and would never return to England again. Looking round her bedroom, Elinor hoped that she was here to stay too. It was such a beautiful room, of majestic proportions, and fitted with her own small bathroom and shower. But, best of all, it looked over the courtyard down below, the heart of the whole house, so that the smell of the flowers came in on the gentle wind and she could look out and see the song-birds her father kept there, dancing in the dappled sun.

'We'll dine whenever you're ready, Elinor,' her father called up to her.

She gave her hands a perfunctory wash and wished that she had not shared this particular room with Zachary. Not that it mattered, she told her reflection earnestly, because she wouldn't think about it again.

A small noise behind her made her turn round and she saw that a small Berber maid had come in to turn down her bed.

'Aïlla!' she greeted her joyfully, and kissed her firmly on both cheeks. Aïlla tried to hide the tattoo marks that disfigured her face, just as she always had, and Elinor prevented her, because she was rather proud of the intricate blue lines that Aïlla's parents had believed would bring their daughter good luck and a wealthy husband.

'You mustn't hide your face,' Elinor said gravely. 'We need all that good luck, don't you think?'

'In this house we do!' Aïlla giggled. 'Now get along with you, Miss Elinor, the cook has swordfish on the menu for you tonight!'

'And what else?' Elinor asked, pleased that the servants should have remembered her favourites.

'*Couscous.* He wouldn't serve anything else, your first day home and hungry for Moroccan food!' the maid teased her.

21

The meal was served in the courtyard. Her father brought out the ancient candlesticks and lit the candles which filled the whole patio with their golden light, making flickering shadows that flattered all their looks and brought an aura of contentment to the three of them. The marble flooring reflected the soft light and the birds, long since asleep, woke up and fluttered a sleepy greeting before returning to their perches and sleep.

Elinor looked across at the two men opposite her.

'It seems so long since I last ate out here!' she said.

Gerard Roche smiled at her.

'I can't say the same,' he said. 'I'm here so often that I sometimes think your father may wonder if I have a home to go to. Not that I have much of a place! Anyway, it certainly hasn't been the same without you, has it, sir?'

Her father smiled sadly at Elinor.

'No. It has never been the same since you first went to England determined to become a nurse. Welcome home, daughter! This time I can say it to you. This time it is going to be different—with no complications!' His eyes slid significantly to the young man beside him and back to his daughter. 'The business I have built up is growing daily. I should like to see it securely established in the family before I die.'

'But that won't be for years yet!' Elinor said cheerfully.

Her father gave her an irritated look. 'It may be sooner than you think!' he growled. 'It takes a long time to settle these things.'

Elinor looked at him and laughed. 'I believe this is some conspiracy!' she teased him. 'It's too bad of you to make fun of me!'

Mr. Kendon shook his head. 'These things come about despite the wishes of old men!' he told her. 'You can't go on mourning for ever!'

Elinor blinked. How could she explain, she wondered, that she was no longer mourning for Zachary? She was a different person now, with a different life to lead, and she had faced that fact. She looked across at Gerard Roche and was surprised to see that he was the one who was blushing.

'But can't you see, I'm quite happy as I am!' she protested to them both.

The young Frenchman sighed eagerly. 'I'm happy too!' he said. 'Now that you've come home.'

He laughed, and Elinor found herself laughing with him. It was fun to have someone to flirt with after all this time.

Elinor thought that if she was to find a job she ought to start looking at once. She knew how easy it would be to fall in with her father's ways, to run his house for him and to forget that she ought to be living her own life and earning her own living.

'I shall try all the hospitals,' she said to Gerard.

He nodded quietly. 'Why don't you work for your father?' he asked. 'We could do with a sort of district nurse to sort out our workers. Some of them don't even realise when they are sick.'

But her father was against the idea.

'I want Elinor to have a bit of a holiday,' he maintained stubbornly. 'Why don't you take some time off too, Gerard? It will be more fun for you to go about together.'

The Frenchman had looked first of all surprised and then pleased. 'I'd like it!' he agreed.

Elinor wasn't quite so sure, but somehow or other it all seemed to be arranged, and she didn't like to disappoint Gerard who was obviously looking forward to something like a prolonged holiday.

'But sooner or later I must get a job,' she said finally.

'When you've got used to being home,' her father agreed smoothly. 'There's lots of time.'

Truly it seemed as if there were. Elinor was more glad than she could say to be back in Morocco. It was not only that it was here that she had grown up, it was also that she was more tired than she had thought after the last hectic rush at the hospital in England and it was rather nice to have time to please herself and to do what she wanted to.

'Perhaps I'll take a couple of weeks' holiday,' she mused.

Gerard Roche grinned at her. 'Done!' he said.

They celebrated by going out to dinner the following evening. Gerard, a true Frenchman, knew of a particular restaurant which he thought she would like.

'I only discovered it recently,' he told her. 'It isn't smart at all, but it has the finest chef in Meknes.'

He called for her in the car, complaining about the narrow streets and the difficulty of driving a car in a land where most of the people either walked or rode on donkeys.

'They just ignore the motor car as if it wasn't there!' he complained. 'And as for turning the thing in these streets——!'

Elinor laughed. 'You should walk like everyone else,' she said. 'I ride a bicycle sometimes——'

Gerard gave her a look of horror. 'Are you fooling? Can you *see* me on a bicycle?'

She had to confess that it was an unlikely spectacle. Gerard was the sort of man who needed a car to complete him. He was self-assured and apparently prosperous, and yet there was a great deal of the little boy lost about him.

'What brought you to Morocco?' she asked him.

He looked engagingly frank.

'The money as much as anything. I was doing all right in France, but I thought I could do a great deal better here. I can too—but it gets lonely sometimes.'

'Lonely?' Elinor could hardly believe him. It had seemed to her that Moroccan life was too social, too friendly, for anyone ever to be lonely.

'I've found it so,' he said. 'I spend a lot of my time on my own. It's different if one is married and has a home.'

'I suppose so,' she said doubtfully.

'Didn't you find it so?' he asked her.

24

'I wasn't married long enough to find out!' she said coldly. She didn't want to talk about Zachary any more, and even less did she want to talk about herself.

'I suppose so,' Gerard agreed calmly. He smiled at her. 'Your loss is my gain!' he said with some satisfaction. 'It wouldn't have been at all the same if you were married now, would it?'

It was easy, she discovered, to fall in with his gentle laughter. In Gerard's company nothing seemed to matter very much and nobody ever got hurt. It was something that she could appreciate, and she was grateful to him for making her feel a woman again and a pretty one at that!

The restaurant he had chosen was French in outlook and design. The head waiter led them to a small secluded table, bowing all the way.

'We are honoured, *madame, monsieur*. Please come this way. I think you will like this table, no? From here you can see the cabaret well. I will send the waiter at once.' He disappeared back towards the door, a single lifted finger bringing two or three waiters running to their table.

Elinor sat down and looked round the room. The restaurant was crowded and, by the look of expectation in the eyes of the patrons, an excellent cabaret was to be expected.

'Elinor darling——'

Elinor started. *Darling* indeed! She frowned across the table at Gerard, not at all sure that she liked him to be so familiar.

'I'm sorry,' he said gently, 'but that is the way I think of you.'

'I can't think why!' she retorted grimly. 'You scarcely know me!'

He smiled and she was more than ever aware of his mockery.

'I don't think time has very much to do with it,' he suggested. 'Has it?'

When appealed to like that, she had to admit that it

25

didn't. It hadn't with her and Zachary. They had taken one look at each other and that had been enough. But she didn't feel like that now. She was glad to have Gerard's company and it was nice to know that he found her attractive, but she had not meant to get in any deeper than that.

'I think perhaps time has quite a lot to do with me now,' she said, sadly. 'I need time.' She hesitated. 'Do you mind?' she asked almost humbly.

He shook his head. 'I can wait,' he said. He laughed with a confidence that she didn't quite like. 'I haven't much competition, have I?'

She blushed. 'Perhaps not,' she admitted abruptly.

He was immediately contrite. 'But, darling, can't you see how glad I am to have you to myself? You might not see me in a crowd and then where should I be?'

Elinor stirred uncomfortably.

'What do you really want?' she asked him in a tight voice. She would have liked to have sounded indifferent and sophisticated, but somehow she couldn't, and she was afraid of her own gaucheness and lack of experience.

'I want marriage,' Gerard admitted frankly.

She was startled. 'With me?'

'Why not?'

She licked her lips which had suddenly gone dry. Marriage! But he was a stranger to her. She didn't know him at all and he certainly didn't know her! There were things that she needed and things which she had done which he wouldn't understand at all. She would need time, and lots of it, in which to make up her mind, she thought. It had all been so different before, but perhaps there had been less of her for Zachary to know. She had been so young two years before, but now she was as old as the hills.

'Why not?' she repeated. 'Because I've been married before. One can't just pretend it never happened!'

'I'm not!' he protested. 'But it was over so quickly that it hardly seems to count.' He made a slight face, aware that he was not making matters any better. 'You *must* know what I mean!'

'Yes, I do,' she agreed slowly. She suspected that she was being difficult and hard to please. He was doing all he could to appeal to her and she was just ungrateful and stupid. Bravely, she smiled at him.

'I'm terribly flattered,' she told him gamely. 'And I like you—a lot! But I must have more time——' She had to have time to close that chapter of her life that she had lived with Zachary, because it had to be completely closed, finally, once and for all, before she could agree to making up her mind to anything else.

'I'll give you all the time you want!' he exclaimed eagerly. 'I don't want to hurry you. I want you to think about it and let the idea grow inside you until you want it as much as I do——'

His enthusiasm was completely endearing. Elinor looked into his eyes and thought what a long time it had been since she had gone out with any man just to enjoy herself. And Gerard was nice, as nice as her father had said he was. But the thought of her father made her frown. It was a cynical thought, she knew, but how much was Gerard acting for himself and how much on her father's instructions?

'We'll do this often!' Gerard insisted. 'Won't we?'

And Elinor felt ashamed of herself for doubting his motives. She smiled back at him.

'Often!' she agreed, and lifted her glass to seal the bargain.

Elinor slept very little that night. To begin with, she was strangely excited. All thoughts of marriage had been so far away from her thoughts for so long that now they seemed doubly attractive. She did not want to live her whole life alone. Other people did so with dignity, even from choice, but she knew that it was not for her. She needed the warmth and colour of marriage, and she wanted children and all that went with them.

So why not marry Gerard, she reflected, as he was there and agreeable? And yet that didn't seem a very good basis for marriage either. She wished she knew how much he liked her and how much he was trying to please her father. She tossed and turned the night away and was just as un-decided in the morning. It was only when she was getting dressed that she admitted to herself that she was flattered and felt truly alive for the first time in two years because Gerard Roche had smiled at her. And she liked him. She liked him very much, and if she didn't love him yet, she was sure that she soon would. She was sure of that. It would please so many people if she did.

Her father was already eating his breakfast in the court-yard when she went downstairs. He looked up at her and she was embarrassed by the frank curiosity in his eyes.

'Did you have a good evening?' he asked.

She was deliberately non-committal. She shrugged her shoulders and smiled.

'It was fun,' she said casually.

Her father jerked upright. 'No more than that?' he demanded.

'What more do you expect?' she retorted.

Mr. Kendon sighed.

'I suppose I don't have to tell you that it would give me great happiness to see you properly settled? I'm not as young as I was, you know——' His voice trailed off and Elinor cast him a quick, anxious look. His face was grey and little lines of weariness had etched themselves into his face around the eyes.

'I know,' she said gently. 'But these things take time.'

He nodded, looking unaccountably sad, and patted her arm.

'I know, dear, I know. But old men grow impatient and can't wait for ever.'

Elinor ate her breakfast without giving a thought to what

she ate. She had been home such a short time and already the pressures were building up on her to do this and that. She was genuinely disturbed about her father's health and she wanted badly to please him the next time she got married. It would have been nice, though, if she could have sat back and enjoyed being courted, without any hurry to make up her mind, or to rush into marriage with a comparative stranger. She would have liked to have had the fun without the cares and the worries of being made up to a little.

She sighed, and her father looked up and smiled.

'Oh well,' he said, 'at one time I never thought I'd have you opposite me again at the breakfast table as my own daughter. That's enough for me at the moment. There's no hurry for anything else.'

But there was, Elinor thought, because she herself couldn't go on for long in a state of suspense, being pulled and pushed this way and that.

'It will all work out in the end,' she said, more to reassure herself than her father. 'Meanwhile, I just want to enjoy being back home.'

'Of course,' Mr. Kendon agreed smoothly.

It was a distressing day. Elinor reproached herself first for being disloyal to Zachary, and then laughed at herself for being so foolish as not to jump at the chance of marrying Gerard.

'You are looking pale,' Aïlla, her maid, told he when she had gone to her room to escape the two men down below.

Elinor smiled bleakly. 'I can't make up my mind——' she began to explain.

The maid sniffed. 'It is none of my business, but,' she began in the manner of family servants the whole world over, 'it seems to me that your time in England was no good to you at all!'

'Why not?' Elinor cried out, surprised by this unexpected attack.

Aïlla gave her a look of affectionate contempt.

'You're no nearer forgetting Zachary than you ever were!' she said baldly. 'No matter how many men there are down there wanting to marry you!' she added, taking base advantage of Elinor's surprised silence.

'I don't know how you can say so!' Elinor stammered at last. 'I've a good mind to go down there and tell Gerard I'll marry him right now!'

Aïlla frowned at her. The good luck markings on her face shone very blue in the light from the window and her eyes glittered dangerously.

'You'd be a fool!' she said sharply.

Elinor turned and faced her. 'Maybe,' she admitted. 'Only time will tell!'

She slipped out of the dress she was wearing and flung it carelessly across the bed. Deliberately she went over to the wardrobe and chose one of the dresses that she had left behind when she had gone to England.

'You're never going to wear that!' Aïlla pleaded with her. 'You haven't worn it since——'

'It may be a little old-fashioned,' Elinor retorted, grimly struggling into the dress, 'but wear it I shall!' She twitched the skirts into position and zipped up the placket. 'I can't live in the past for ever, can I?'

The maid shook her head anxiously.

'Is it your father who has persuaded you?' she whispered. 'It should be your own decision—no one else's!'

Elinor chuckled without amusement. 'How many of your people can choose?' she demanded. 'And yet it often works out very well, doesn't it?'

Aïlla pursed up her lips and refused to reply. Elinor stood, almost in tears, waiting for an answer for a long moment, but the maid resolutely turned her back and began to clear up the room. With dragging feet, Elinor turned to go downstairs with all the resolution she could muster. Anything, she told herself fiercely, was better than indecision. It had to be. But even so it seemed a long way down to the courtyard below.

The two men looked up to greet her.

'You're looking very pretty!' Gerard exclaimed, leaping to his feet.

Elinor, who was quite aware that the glint of temper became her, was unimpressed. She smiled at him carefully and sat down in the chair he dragged across the courtyard for her.

'What are you drinking?' she asked him, aware of her father's interested gaze.

'Fruit juice,' Gerard laughed. 'Very innocuous!'

'I think I'll have one too,' she said casually.

She tried to pretend that she didn't notice when he brought his own chair nearer hers. She even tried to pretend to herself that his attentions gave her active pleasure, and perhaps they did, because he certainly looked very eager and handsome—and *young*! He made her feel old and experienced, but she tried to ignore the sensation.

'This is very pleasant,' she said aloud. 'I'm glad I'm not working yet. I have the most delicious idle feeling!'

Gerard laughed at her. 'How nice!' he teased her. He handed her his glass so that she wouldn't have to wait for her own drink. 'I've drunk out of the glass!' he reminded her, looking like a small boy. 'Just there!'

She wondered if she were expected to drink from the same place and thought sadly that her ability to flirt successfully seemed to have taken a nose-dive. Fortunately she was saved from actually having to drink anything because there was a sudden commotion in the hall and the sounds of physical combat.

'What on earth is that?' she asked blankly.

Her father rose slowly to his feet and half-stumbled as his legs took his full weight. He had aged so very much since she had last seen him, she thought blankly. She wished that Gerard would go and find out what all the noise was and save her father even those few steps. But the

Frenchman had slouched back into his chair and was taking no further interest in the proceedings. Mr. Kendon balanced himself and took a step forward, just as an Arab burst his way into the courtyard and fell at the older man's feet.

His headdress hid his face as he struggled to his feet. Elinor rose swiftly to aid him and was shocked by the slightness of the arm beneath her fingers. At that moment he brushed the grimy cloth out of his face and stood, silently looking at her. She could feel the blood slowly leaving her face.

'Zachary!' she whispered.

CHAPTER THREE

ELINOR was quite sure that she was going to faint. Only one did not faint in these modern days. She stared at Zachary with increasing bewilderment. The shock had drained the strength from her limbs and she could only stand and continue to look unbelievingly at him.

'Zachary!' she said faintly.

He smiled at her rather grimly.

'In person,' he said at last. His accent was so startlingly familiar and yet so acute to her unaccustomed ears that she could have cried. She began to look at him more carefully and was shocked to see how his eyes had fallen into his head and the weariness that was etched on his face like a mask.

'Wherever have you been?' she asked inadequately.

He put his hand up to shelter his eyes.

'Does it matter?' he asked wearily. 'Aren't you going to welcome me home?'

But she could not. She was shy of him as she never had been before and she was uncertain of everything, himself included.

'I expect you're hungry,' she said inadequately, twisting her hands together to avoid having to look at him.

For the first time Walter Kendon addressed his son-in-law.

'Don't you consider that you owe us an explanation at all?' he demanded. Zachary gave him a sardonic smile, looking first at Elinor and then at Gerard Roche, his eyebrows rising a trifle.

'I suppose I do,' he drawled. 'But I'll give one to my wife in the privacy of our own room. In the meantime I'm both hungry and tired.'

Walter Kendon looked decidedly put out.

'There's no room for you in my house,' he said abruptly. 'You may stay for lunch, but that's all!'

Zachary turned his whole attention away from Mr. Kendon and back to Elinor.

'I gather that you've missed me?' he said ironically.

Elinor drew herself up abruptly. How would she ever be able to explain to this stranger how much she had missed him? How often she had cried herself to sleep and how long it had taken for that numb feeling of despair to leave her? But this wasn't the same man! This was a stranger she had never met before, who was so thin that he looked scarcely more substantial than a skeleton.

'I did at first. I got over it—one has to!' she said in a tight, nervous voice.

Zachary looked at her for a long moment. She was aware of the almost pleading look in his eyes, but she couldn't get over the awful embarrassment that gripped her, nor could she quite believe that this was the man she had known and married—he looked so different! So much less glamorous!

'Well,' he said slowly, 'this is hardly the welcome that Odysseus received!' He glanced across at Gerard Roche. 'Who is he?' he asked. 'One of Penelope's suitors?'

'Zachary!' Elinor protested. The first shock of his arrival was beginning to wear off and she was very close to tears.

Gerard Roche stood to attention and bowed slightly.

'I am very proud to serve Miss Kendon in any way I am able!' he said stiffly.

Zachary managed a laugh.

'I thought so! But she happens to be Mrs. Wild! Or had you all forgotten?'

'That can be remedied!' Walter Kendon put in sharply. 'She was too young to know what she was doing! You can't waltz in and out of people's lives like that and expect them to be the same as when you left. Your claims are over now!'

Zachary turned to Elinor, grasping her arm until it hurt. She wished that he didn't look so painfully tired and that

34

he would kiss her and get it over with. Couldn't he see how strange she felt? He was thin too, she noticed. Thin and hard and his fingernails were dirty.

'Is it over, Elinor?' he asked her.

She looked in vain for any gentleness in him. With the back of one hand she brushed away a tear as it slid down her cheek.

'We—we could have the marriage annulled,' she suggested faintly, bitterly aware of the triumph on her father's face.

For the first time his smile looked more like the Zachary she had known and loved. She found herself blushing at his look and hastily looked away from him.

'Not annulled!' he said softly. 'Our marriage was scarcely a figment of my imagination!'

Elinor blushed again. What little hold she felt she had had over events was fast evaporating. But then she felt Zachary sway against her. How could they all have been so selfish? she wondered bitterly. He was dropping on his feet and all they could do was to stand round and argue. There would be time enough for that when he had eaten and slept.

'Sit down, do, Zachary!' she bade him. 'We'll have lunch straight away and then you can sleep!'

Obediently he collapsed into the chair she had just vacated.

'I'm sorry to be such a nuisance,' he muttered.

Elinor shook her head. She felt very much happier now she had something definite to do.

'I'll have the food brought immediately,' she promised. She clapped her hands to summon the servants. But her father's butler had already seen Zachary come and came running in, his eyes shining, to set the food on the already laid table.

Mr. Kendon rose slowly and went to the table.

'Do you intend to sit down and eat with us before you've even washed?' he asked Zachary tetchily.

Zachary stood up, still swaying slightly from fatigue.

'I'm sorry,' he said. 'I've almost forgotten what it's like to be clean——'

'Well, we haven't!' Mr. Kendon retorted.

Elinor pulled Zachary hastily into a chair, very much the nurse who would brook no defiance.

'You're too tired to do anything but eat something and go straight to bed!' she said with the whole weight of her training behind her. 'Eat up, Zachary, and I'll get Aïlla to make up a bed for you!'

He smiled gratefully at her. 'Thank you,' he said, and he sounded as if he meant it. 'Thank you very much.'

Zachary ate everything in sight, though he was so tired that little could have made much sense to him. Elinor gave him a worried glance as he almost fell over the table, but he recovered himself and smiled hazily across the table at her.

'I was in such a hurry to get home!' he confided to her. 'I can't think why now! You don't care, do you?'

Elinor thought that she could hardly tell him that she was feeling nothing at all. That she didn't *know* what she felt. She had remembered him for so long in agony that she couldn't really believe that he was walking around and talking to her. He seemed more like a phantom come to mock her.

'At least you'll have a comfortable bed and some food inside you!' she said sharply.

He looked at the steaming plate of *couscous* that had been placed in the centre of the table, looking hungrily at the lumps of meat and vegetables that garnished the main ingredient.

'Too right!' he said nastily. 'I've been living on next to nothing for weeks,' he added.

Elinor winced as if it were her own hunger she was feeling. His face was so terribly bony and she could practically see his ribs when his robe fell apart to reveal the tight shirt he was wearing underneath. She bit her lip. She wished urgently that she had the strength to welcome him whole-heartedly and to forget all about her own doubts and difficulties. Perhaps she had no right even to expect an explanation so soon and in such circumstances?

Mr. Kendon eyed his son-in-law across the table with unconcealed hostility.

'I imagine it was all your own fault!' he stated finally.

Zachary gave a gasping laugh. 'I suppose in a way it was,' he admitted. He put down his knife and fork and looked wildly round the courtyard. 'I'm awfully sorry,' he said, 'but I don't think I can stay awake any longer!'

Elinor clapped her hands and Aïlla, never far from her mistress when she was in Morocco, came running into the courtyard.

'Show Dr. Wild to a bed,' Elinor bade her gently.

Aïlla's dark eyes met hers in surprise. 'But——' she began.

Zachary snorted with laughter and pointed an accusing finger at Elinor.

'You see! I'm not the only one to think that a more wifely welcome is my due!'

Elinor blushed scarlet.

'I can't!' she said abruptly. 'It's been too long—I don't feel that I know you at all!'

His eyes met hers and once again she was tempted to risk everything and fling herself into his arms. But he gave her no opportunity to do anything of the sort. He turned away and followed Aïlla into the house, chatting away to her in the Moroccan dialect of Arabic that she understood much better than either English or French. Apparently what he had to say was amusing, because Aïlla giggled and gave Gerard Roche a faintly hostile look as she went past him. Weakly, and with a feeling of utter failure, Elinor remembered how the servants had always liked Zachary. She sighed and smiled determinedly at her father and Gerard, but neither of them made any attempt to smile back.

'I hope he'll be all right,' she said with a brightness that told her how near to tears she really was. 'Do you think I should go with him?'

'Certainly not!' her father grunted. 'A most unwelcome surprise!'

'Oh, how can you say so?' she appealed to him, more hurt than she liked to admit.

'Only too easily,' he replied. 'You should never have married such an adventurer in the first place. I had hoped that he was dead, but as it seems we were all mistaken about that, we must take steps to set you free of him.' He looked at her in quite a kindly manner. 'It will be by far the best thing, my dear. I shouldn't suggest it otherwise. But you couldn't continue with such a marriage, never knowing when he would disappear again! Never even knowing whether he was alive or dead! It would be quite impossible to bring up children in those circumstances, especially children who would eventually have to take over all that I've built up out here! No, no, quite impossible!'

Elinor said nothing. She felt a strong inclination to go to her room and have a nice cry, but she knew it wouldn't really solve anything, so she stood her ground.

'I'll think about it, Father,' she said.

And so the arguments went on all day while Zachary slept. Mr. Kendon and Gerard joined forces to explain to Elinor how mistaken she would be if she were to stay with her husband.

'If he hadn't broken your heart this way, he would soon have chosen some other way to do so!' her father insisted.

'Women?' Gerard asked succinctly.

Mr. Kendon nodded.

'Far too charming for it to have been otherwise!' he reached across and took Elinor's hand in his. 'It's been a long, tiring day for you, my dear. Why don't you have an early night and leave the whole affair for your father to sort out for you?'

Elinor nodded, even though she was still unconvinced.

'I suppose it is the best thing to do,' she agreed wearily. 'I hope you will both excuse me?' she added formally, and went into the house. But she had not gone before she could hear Gerard's whispered question to her father as to how the marriage had come about. She would have to get used to people talking behind her back, she told herself dismally. From now on they would be whispering wherever she went. And it would always be about her and Zachary and how he had come to leave her after such a short time of marriage. She had lived through it all before and she couldn't bear to do so again! It was his turn to suffer from malicious and wounding tongues, and she wouldn't help him one bit! More, she would even enjoy it, so she couldn't think why she was so miserable! It hurt her too to think how much he had changed. She knew now that she had spent the last two years mourning a complete stranger.

Ailla left Elinor to sleep in the morning. At intervals she put her head round the door to see if her mistress was stirring, but the sun was high in the heavens before Elinor sleepily stretched herself and struggled into a sitting position to see the time.

'Ailla!' she called.

The maid came running into the room.

'Breakfast?' she asked, her smile showing that she knew how shocked Elinor would be to find how late it was.

'It depends——' Elinor began uncertainly. 'Did Dr. Wild sleep well?' she asked.

Ailla sniffed.

'I hadn't thought you were interested,' she said, her voice stiff with disapproval.

Elinor blinked. 'Of course I'm interested. You know I am! Only his arrival was so unexpected and Father was so displeased to see him!'

'And so was his wife!' Ailla added.

Elinor blushed. 'I don't feel like his wife any more,' she explained, and wished she didn't have to try. Aïlla had known her since she was a little girl, but it didn't really give her the right to question her actions now. 'I suppose I ought to go and have a talk to him,' she said with what dignity she could muster.

Aïlla sniffed again.

'The doctor has already left the house,' she told Elinor.

'Left? But where for?'

'Where? To his own dwelling! Why should he remain here?' Aïlla asked her reasonably. 'He will want to be at home to his friends.'

Elinor stared at her maid. It wasn't the ideal way of finding out what Zachary was doing, she supposed, but obviously all the servants knew much more about him than she did.

'He hasn't got a house!' she protested. 'He—we always lived here. I mean, after we were married.'

'That was for the honeymoon,' Aïlla smiled. 'Sure the doctor has a house!'

'Where is it?' Elinor asked her almost timidly.

But Aïlla would only shake her head.

'He will tell you when he is ready,' she said comfortably. 'Sit up now and I will fetch your breakfast.'

Elinor watched the maid depart with an expression of resentment. There was no possible reason that she could see why she shouldn't be told Zachary's address. There were things they had to discuss, arrangements to be made. They had to get to know each other again, and anyway she wanted to hear what had happened to him and where he had been these long two years.

But Aïlla was just as firm when she came back carrying the *café complet* that Elinor always had for her breakfast.

'If I wrote a note——' Elinor suggested thoughtfully.

Aïlla shook her head.

'He will call on you when he is ready.' For an instant her

eyes looked sad. 'You had your chance to speak with him last night, but you were too proud to take it!'

'It wasn't like that!' Elinor said desperately.

'To him it seemed that way!' Ailla retorted. 'But you will do yourself no good to worry about it all now. Besides, Monsieur Roche is waiting for you in the patio.'

Elinor made a face. 'What does he want?' she asked crossly.

Ailla shrugged her shoulders.

'With him, I wouldn't know,' she answered enigmatically. She smiled suddenly. 'It is not the way I would wish, but it is good to have you home again! You have become pale in England, but soon the sun will bring your skin to perfection and you will have much more to say to Dr. Wild!'

'If I ever find out where he lives!' Elinor retorted nastily.

'He knows where you live!' Ailla pointed out. 'He will come when he is ready!'

Elinor swallowed her coffee and buttered one of the hot rolls, eyeing her maid as she did so.

'If you say that just once again——' she threatened.

Ailla laughed. 'That's just as I thought!' she said mildly. 'You coming home yourself so recently and not having time to settle in properly has left you not knowing whether you are on your head or your heels. Your father may think that from now on you will do as he says, but I know you better than that! Is that coffee hot enough?'

Elinor poured herself out some more and nearly burned her mouth as she sipped it.

'Yes, thank you, it's too hot! But you're wrong, Ailla. One time I might have gone my own way, but it wasn't very successful for any of us, was it? My father may be right, you know. He may be the better judge of character and I may be much happier with his choice!'

Ailla said nothing. She pursed up her mouth and went

41

about the room unnecessarily clearing Elinor's things away, moving her clothes from one chair to another and back again.

'I gather you don't agree?' Elinor said to her uncompromising back.

'It's none of my business!' the maid retorted. 'What you suggest is no more than what has been the custom in this country since time began. Why should I say it is wrong?'

'But you think it is?'

Aïlla approached the bed, looking almost threatening, though all she did was to pick up the breakfast tray.

'I think it is too late to think about these things!' she said finally. 'You are not a young girl any longer. You are already married to Dr. Wild!'

'But that could be changed!' Elinor replied unhappily.

'By whom?' the maid asked her. 'By you? By your father?'

Elinor nodded. 'It would be so much better!' she insisted. 'I was so unhappy!'

Aïlla's expression softened.

'He knows that! Never you fear, he understands how you feel. Does the other one?'

Elinor sighed. 'I don't know,' she said frankly.

When Aïlla had gone, Elinor got up and dressed herself carefully before going downstairs and out into the patio.

'Good morning!' she greeted Gerard Roche.

He rose from the seat he had found in a shady corner in one corner of the patio. He wasn't particularly tall and in her high-heeled shoes, Elinor could look him straight in the eyes.

'Hullo,' he said. 'I hope you don't mind my calling so early? Your father suggested that you would not like to spend too much time by yourself today.' He managed to look sympathetic and firm at the same time. 'I am going to Fez to visit a dye shop and I thought you might like to accompany me?'

42

Elinor hesitated. What if Zachary should call and find her out? It would be so hard to explain that it wasn't because she didn't want to see him, it was more because she wanted to forget that he had ever come home, because she wasn't ready for the knowledge yet.

'I'd like to,' she said at last.

Gerard smiled at her.

'It's a pretty smelly place—but of course you know that!'

She nodded shyly.

'My father never took me with *him*!' she complained saucily. 'But I have been there. I joined a tourist group once and we went right through the *souks* and everything was explained to us. I've been on my own often since then, but I could never find my way about by myself.'

'You wouldn't be able to,' Gerard agreed. 'I have been going for nearly a year now and I still get lost if I venture away from the path I was first shown.'

Fez was not so very far from Meknes. Gerard drove quickly along the excellent road, smiling now and again as Elinor marvelled at some scene she had practically forgotten in her long absence.

'I'd forgotten the dust and the prickly pear,' she said regretfully at last. 'And the way the sheep and the goats gather together in a single flock. It's all so different in England! Not that I saw much of the countryside. The hospital I was in was right in the heart of London.'

'Why did you go back to England?' Gerard asked curiously.

Elinor frowned with the concentration of finding the right words to tell him.

'I wanted to go away for a while,' she said. 'And I wanted to do something useful. It wasn't easy at first, but I began to forget after a while and I enjoyed my work.'

'And now he's come back?' Gerard inquired gently.

Elinor shrugged. 'I don't know,' she said. 'The servants

43

tell me that he's gone to his own house—I-I didn't even know that he had one! We were married for such a very short time that it all seems more like a dream than anything else!'

'I suppose it would,' the Frenchman agreed. 'Your father would like to keep it that way. You know that?'

Elinor nodded. 'Yes, I know that,' she said painfully. 'You see, he never did like Zachary much.'

Gerard frowned at the road ahead.

'I don't suppose they have much in common,' he said pacifically. 'Your father eats, breathes and lives his work, doesn't he?'

Elinor looked out of the window. 'So did Zachary!' she said, carefully keeping any expression out of her voice. 'His work came before everything! A wife was a mere adjunct to him. Not that he ever had time to find out that he had one!'

Gerard whistled under his breath.

'You *were* in love with him, but you didn't like him much, did you?'

Elinor was startled into being completely honest.

'I never really knew him at all!' she exclaimed. 'Can you understand that! He was wonderful and that was that! I don't even know if he takes cream in his coffee!'

Gerard gave her a look of complete satisfaction.

'Then if you'll take uncle's advice,' he said benignly, 'I'd not rush into anything now.'

Elinor grinned at him. 'Not even with you?' she inquired sweetly.

He shook his head reluctantly.

'Not yet. I can wait, my dear. And if I can, your father will have to!'

He really was nice, Elinor thought gratefully.

'You're very kind!' she said. 'And I'll remember your advice. Now, let's forget all about it for the rest of the day!'

44

He grinned at her. 'Suits me!' he said.

Probably the view of Fez, nestling in splendour in its valley, is one of the best-loved and most famous in the world. Elinor had seen it often, but it never failed to stir her imagination. It was poetic, it was majestic and it was very different from the cities she knew in Europe. In this one view lay the whole flavour of Morocco, bearing the romance and the wounds of her history, mysterious and lovely, sad and cruel, and full of warmth and sheer exuberance of North African living.

Gerard stopped the car on the lip of the hill and they got out for a moment to look down at the city stretched out before them. Even from that distance it was possible to hear the hum of the people living and talking below. The noise rose up from the rabbit-warren passageways that made up the local shopping area, known as the *souks*, a mixture of laughter and gossiping tales, bargaining and the harsh Arabic commands that encouraged the laden donkeys along the cobbled alleys.

Without speaking they returned to the car and Gerard drove slowly along the road that went down, almost round the city, and in through the more modern parts where they could leave the car at one of the gates to the *souks*, and go on from there on foot.

'Guide! Good guide! Hire me!' they were invited insistently by a group of men, all bearing the official government seal that proved they were genuine. Gerard laughingly shook his head at them and a few seconds later they had passed through the gate and back through the centuries into the first and most individual city of Fez.

Gerard solemnly counted off the criss-cross alleyways as they passed them so that they would not get lost. Elinor walked after him, stopping every now and again to admire the wares which were on display. Leather goods, carved woods, jewellery of every kind met her eyes. Some of it was cheap and excellent, some of it rather tawdry, but all of it was pressed on her, hoping for a sale.

'Come on!' Gerard hurried her on. 'If I don't concentrate we'll lose our way!'

Elinor shivered. She loved the *souks*, but she would not want to be lost in them. They were too mysterious for that. Arabs and Berbers and tribesmen that she couldn't put a name to pressed against her, pushing their way through the alleys, an air of purpose in their eyes.

They came to an intersection and Gerard swore under his breath.

'I can't remember!' he exclaimed angrily.

Elinor looked about her anxiously. To her surprise a tall man came forward and beckoned to her.

'Take the third street on your right,' he whispered to her.

She thanked him, without wondering how he should know where they wanted to go. And then she looked at him again. For a moment she could have sworn that it was Zachary. But that was ridiculous! Zachary would be at home, probably still sleeping, he had been so tired.

The stranger gave her a quick push in the right direction.

'Zachary!' she pleaded with him, but he didn't hear her, and the next instant he was lost in the crowds again. It had been Zachary! she thought. But what in the world was he doing here?

CHAPTER FOUR

'How do you know which way we ought to go?' Gerard asked her. 'I believe you've been here before—probably a great deal more often than I have!'

'No, truly I haven't,' Elinor assured him. 'It isn't like that at all! A man came out of the crowd back there and told me where to go.'

'Knowing exactly where we're going, I suppose!' Gerard said sarcastically.

'Wasn't it peculiar?' Elinor agreed. 'Do you know, for a moment I thought the man was Zachary! Only of course it couldn't have been. I mean, what would Zachary be doing dressed up as an Arab in Fez?'

'Most unlikely! You've got him on the brain!' Gerard teased her. 'Why don't you forget all about him and enjoy yourself?'

But Elinor was still puzzled by the whole encounter.

'It was a grocer's shop,' she mused aloud. 'At least I think it was.'

'So?' Gerard asked.

'I don't know. I just wondered if the shop was run by one of those tribesmen who came for Zachary in the first place.'

Gerard shrugged. 'Does it matter?' It seemed incredible to Elinor, but Gerard was just not interested in Zachary. She wondered briefly if he was jealous of her erstwhile husband and then laughed at herself for being so vain. Why should Gerard care? He hadn't had time to fall in love with her! It was ambition and her father's wishes that were driving him to court her. And she didn't object, she thought wearily. She had been burned once, badly, and the burned child had very good reason to fear the fire!

47

'No, it doesn't matter,' she said aloud. 'I was probably mistaken anyway.' She looked back down the alleyway along which they had just come. Of course she was mistaken, she thought. Of course she was! It had been silly to even think that it could have been Zachary! As if she wouldn't have recognised that thin bony face at once. There was no forgetting it. Or the haggard, tired look in his eyes. And with determination, she put the idea behind her and followed Gerard along the last few yards to the tannery they were to visit.

They were greeted at the entrance by two men in long robes, with turbans lightly wound around their heads. They bowed, but otherwise were haughtily silent, without a glimmer of a smile disturbing the classic beauty of their faces.

'Welcome to Fez,' the elder said politely.

Elinor waited for Gerard to reply. When he didn't, she answered herself, hoping that they wouldn't mind a woman putting herself forward in such a way.

'May God's blessing rest on you in this house,' she muttered.

A smile broke across the older man's face.

'So! You know a little of our language?' he asked her.

She nodded. 'I try to learn a little, but I'm afraid I'm not a very good student. I find it very difficult,' she admitted.

'But nevertheless, it is a good thing to try,' he praised her. 'You must both come inside and my wife will bring us some mint tea. It is hot wandering through the *souks* if one is not accustomed to it.'

Elinor had been prepared for the ceremony of drinking tea even if it had been ice-cold outside. Gerard, however, was more impatient. She tried to throw him a warning look, knowing how little Moroccans like to be bustled out of what they consider to be good manners.

'Miss Kendon is the daughter of my employer,' he told them. 'She has lived here on and off ever since she was a child.'

48

The Moroccans snubbed him gently.

'We have met Miss Kendon before. Once before she came with her father, but she was too young to remember very much about it. It is a pleasure to welcome her once again.'

They led the way inside, quite at home in the splendid atmosphere in which they lived. The building could have come straight out of the Arabian Nights, it was so elaborate and of such magnificent proportions. They were taken into a fairly small reception room, where there were a few embroidered cushions on the floor, and one or two low occasional tables carved intricately out of sweet-smelling sandalwood.

Elinor sat down on one of the cushions, curling her feet in under her in a way she had almost forgotten. She almost giggled when she saw the trouble Gerard was having and was amused by the solemn winks the Arabs gave her. They too were amused by the look of intense discomfort on Gerard's face.

'My name is Brahim,' the elder Moroccan introduced himself. 'This is my son Abdullah.'

Elinor bowed politely. She wished more urgently that Gerard would play his proper part in the conversation, for she knew that neither of these two men would find it seemly if she were to speak too much.

Brahim clapped his hands and a veiled woman entered the room and placed a copper tray on the rug before him. On it was a chased silver tea-pot of which the family was obviously enormously proud. There were also three other silver boxes, a small flat hammer, and several coloured glasses. A few seconds later another woman entered bringing a minute kettle boiling on a charcoal brazier.

'This is very kind of you,' Gerard said restively. 'But really we ought to get started on our work. Couldn't we have this tea when we've finished?'

Brahim shook his head. 'The young lady is tired. It is

well she should be refreshed before we start to go round the tannery. Business is not for women!'

Gerard laughed. 'You'd be surprised!' he said cynically.

Brahim's mouth twitched sympathetically.

'Perhaps, but it is not a good thing for them to know,' he replied flatly. 'Now tell me how you found your way here this time?'

Gerard frowned, not wanting to be reminded of their walk through the *souks*.

'I got lost—as usual!' he sighed. 'But Elinor knew where we were and was able to show me the way.'

Abdullah, much younger than his father and up to now quite silent, looked at Elinor with gleaming eyes.

'You know your way through the *souks*?' he asked her abruptly.

Elinor shook her head.

'No, it was the most peculiar thing. A man, a total stranger, came out of a shop and told me to take the third street on my right. I thought, just for a moment, that he bore a resemblance to Zac—to my husband, but of course I was mistaken!'

'Of course!' Abdullah agreed smoothly.

Brahim turned his head away from the tea-tray.

'Is it true what we hear? That Dr. Wild has come home?'

'Yes,' she murmured. 'Yes, he has come home. But he was too tired yesterday to tell us any of his adventures.'

'And where is he today?' the old man asked by way of rebuke. It was one thing in his eyes for Elinor to have come with Gerard if her husband was dead, quite another if he had come home.

'I don't know,' Elinor said in a whisper.

He looked at her sharply.

'There is time for all things,' he said gently. 'It will be as Allah wills.'

Elinor smiled at him in relief.

50

'Yes,' she agreed thoughtfully, 'all we can do is wait and see.'

Brahim threw some green tea into the tea-pot and poured the boiling water over it. From the second of the silver boxes he produced a loaf of sugar and knocked off a few generous chunks with the hammer. These he forced down the neck of the tea-pot. Then, from the third box, he took some fresh green mint which he pushed in on top of the rest. He closed the lid of the tea-pot with a sigh of pleasure and waited for a minute or so for the tea to draw. Then very carefully he poured a little of the tea into each glass and handed one to each one of his guests.

The sweet, almost syrupy flavour of mint was largely an acquired taste, Elinor remembered. Where she was well known, she had asked, before she had gone away to England and another world, to have her tea before the sugar had been added, but here there was no help for it but to sip her way through the small glass of tea, and through a second, and finally through a third. Then, at last, good manners allowed one to call a halt. She glanced across to see how Gerard was faring and was amused to see how transparent his face was. He was mildly astonished that he should find it so good. He must have a very sweet tooth, she thought, and wondered that he had never been invited to take tea with the Moroccans before. It was so much a part of business that the government had once thought of taking a hand in the business, either by banning it, or by building vast new sugar factories. But that was another story she had never heard the end of.

'You are refreshed, I hope?' Abdullah asked her carefully.

Elinor smiled her gratitude.

'Thanks to your very kind hospitality!' she answered.

Brahim looked satisfied. 'Then now we had better get down to business,' the old man said to Gerard. 'Shall we visit the tannery first to see what skins we have available that will be of interest to you?'

The whole party rose to their feet. Gerard tried unobtrusively shaking the pins and needles out of his feet, and the Moroccans grinned openly at him.

'Next time you come,' they said, 'we shall give you a leather pouffe to sit on. You will find that more comfortable!'

He laughed too. 'I think you'd better,' he said. 'I don't seem to have the knack of sitting on my feet as you do.'

Brahim smiled. 'It will come with much practice, not otherwise.'

The smell of the tannery was abominable. Elinor gasped and struggled and, very gradually, she became more accustomed to the terrible fumes that rose from the enormous concrete basins where they were treating the skins, dyeing them and eventually finishing them ready for the makers of the famous leather goods of Morocco. The dye shop was somewhat better. It was patterned on the same system of a series of oblong baths, none of them quite rectangular, but roughened with much use and the pulling of the skins in and out of the vats when they were heavy and wet. A couple of men stood on the narrow path between the baths, armed with long hooks, and pushed and pulled the skins into the desired colours. Green, scarlet, and a deep purple-blue were the favourite colours, for these responded best to being embossed with gold, but all the browns were represented, and yellow, orange for the more exotic wares and the softest white.

'You have some fine skins here,' Gerard said appreciatively.

Brahim nodded. 'We go right out into the country to find the best,' he said. His eyes rested for an instant on Elinor and his expression was sad. 'Right down in the south, no one is very sure of the boundaries. It is dangerous there sometimes, if you go off the beaten track. There are tribesmen who will have nothing to do with anyone else. They live a harsh life.'

'Oh well,' Gerard said cheerfully, 'they produce some fine animals!'

'Camels and a few head of cattle,' Brahim agreed. 'Mostly they take them into Marrakesh, or one of the other southern towns, and trade there for salt and other necessities. It is the only contact they have with other men.' His eyes fell on Elinor again, thoughtful and still sad.

Gerard rubbed his hands together, warming himself up for the inevitable haggling that accompanied these deals. He would have much preferred to have had a set price, but he knew that the Moroccans would never agree to that. They would want to evaluate each skin individually and marvel at their own labours at turning it into such fine quality leather. They would be there for hours yet and he knew it. But he never enjoyed it, not as Walter Kendon did, his eyes glistening with the battle and his extraordinary pleasure when he knocked a single dirham off the price. Gerard always ended by compromising, bitterly aware of the subtle expression of scorn that came into the tanner's face as he did so.

He began to assess his needs, knowing that most of the leather he was to buy was for pouffes and handbags, such as are familiar in Marrakesh where they often embroider the leather, using festoons of coloured silks or leather thonging. There were *babouches*, a kind of long-toed slipper, and *choukharas*, a type of knapsack worn by almost every man, hung from the shoulder, as a receptacle for their money and papers. But most of all Gerard needed the green and red leathers that were traditional to Fez, to be gilded and turned into bindings for magazines, purses, cigarette cases and a hundred and one other fancy objects for the tourist and local trade.

Elinor lost interest in the bargaining early on. She liked to feel the soft leathers in her hand and conjecture what wonderful things would eventually be made from them, but she was not particularly interested in the mercenary details. She looked at Abdullah, hoping that he too was becoming bored. His quick look of amusement rewarded her.

'You would rather wander in the *souks* with me?' he asked her.

She nodded her head positively.

'Would you mind? My interest in bargaining is non-existent!'

He shook his head at her. 'It is good to save what money one can, don't you think?' he suggested.

She wrinkled up her nose. 'I haven't much ambition,' she said. 'As long as I can make enough to live on, that's all I want. I don't take after my father at all in that respect. He has a very great respect for gold.'

Abdullah laughed.

'All men have! Look at me. I put as much away in the bank as I can manage every day. I want to be a very rich man!'

'And then what will you do with it?' Elinor asked him.

He grinned. 'I shall go to Mecca. To be a Hadji must be the summit of every man's ambition!'

Elinor chuckled.

'My father,' she said dryly, 'is not a Muslim.'

'That is a misfortune,' he agreed in the same dry tone. 'There is obviously nothing for him to spend his riches on!'

Elinor chuckled again. 'Well, it wouldn't be quite the same, would it?' she said.

'No, it would not. For us, to go to Mecca is an honour in which the whole family shares. It is an honour as much as a pilgrimage. It is an event to savour all one's life!'

Elinor was happy to leave the smells of the tannery and go back into the spicy atmosphere of the *souks*. Abdullah led her up and down the busiest markets, explaining how the leather merchants worked the gold on to their leather, and how the metal workers tapped at their metals to produce the gorgeous silver and copper plates that were on sale

54

everywhere, tempting the tourist to spend his all in a single morning or afternoon.

'You could live your whole life in the *souks*,' Abdullah told her, 'and not lack for anything.'

He showed her the oldest university in the world, where she could only stand in the entrance and peer into the courtyard beyond. One or two young Moors ran in and out, their serious expressions showing that their study of the Koran, the holy book of Islam, was not to be taken lightly. Others, perhaps younger, found the whole of life a gay and exciting affair and their laughter could be heard above the hum of the *souks*, as they chased one another through the narrow, covered streets, sure-footed in the dappled light despite the uneven cobblestones and the sudden rises and falls in the level of the street.

There were grocers galore. Their small shops bulged with so many varieties of goods that a supermarket would seem tame by comparison. The owner would stand in the small space in the centre, apparently never bothering to shut his doors, catering for every desire that anyone could have. Mostly he even slept in his shop so as to be always there, even if a customer should come late at night or early in the morning.

'What a life!' Elinor said with feeling, as Abdullah recounted their hours of work and the way in which they lived.

Abdullah shrugged. 'They have their eyes on better things,' he said indifferently. 'Most of them only come here to get enough money to buy land in their own area down south.'

A feeling of excitement stirred Elinor.

'Are they all Chleuhs?' she asked him.

'Mostly. They're a strange people. They come to the cities detemined that their services will make them rich. Usually it does! Now and again a 'banker', someone they really trust, will come to their shop and they will give him all the money they have. This will go down to Tafraout, or near there, to buy land and stock. Later, when the man is rich, he will go down to the home he has bought there, probably taking a fine modern car with him.'

'But Tafraout isn't so very remote, is it?' Elinor said. 'A lot of tourists want to see the most southerly town in Morocco, surely?'

'Some of them do. But the country round there is practically unexplored. The Chleuhs share the extreme south with the blue men. Nothing will make them see civilisation as an advantage. Not even money! They raise a few camels and keep themselves to themselves. I don't think even the government interferes with them much.'

'And do they have many dealings with the Chleuh?' Elinor asked.

Abdullah shook his head.

'I couldn't say! I've never been there. Fez is my world. I seldom leave the city unless I have to.'

Elinor looked thoughtful. 'I think I'd like to go there—some time,' she said slowly. 'Just to see what it's like!'

Abdullah laughed. 'As long as you don't expect me to go with you!' he teased her. 'I don't suppose,' he added on a note of mischievous fun, 'your father or Gerard would enjoy the trip much either!'

Elinor smiled at the thought. 'I suppose not!' she said.

They wandered slowly back through the labyrinth of narrow streets back to the tannery. Occasionally a donkey would push its way past them and every now and then a party of tourists, complete with official guide, would stop at carefully selected shops and would admire the goods for sale and try to get the guide to argue about the prices for them.

Gerard and Brahim were waiting for them when they got back to the tannery. Judging by the look of complete satisfaction on both men's faces they had done good business together and Gerard would be back later on to buy more

56

skins to feed the insatiable appetite of the business Walter Kendon had created.

Elinor looked over the pile of leathers that had been put on one side.

'Will Father be pleased, do you think?' she asked Gerard.

'Delighted!' he assured her. 'We've done even better than I hoped.'

Brahim smiled wisely at them both. 'It is the only good way to do business,' he said. 'To have both the buyer and the seller well satisfied.'

He and Abdullah seemed genuinely sad to have them depart. Abdullah came with them to the main gate of the Medina and pointed across to the car park where Gerard had left his car.

'Another time I will show you the best way to come to us,' he promised. 'I can easily meet you here at the main gate.'

'Thank you very much.'

They all shook hands and Abdullah bowed and made a graceful gesture with his hand to show that what he said came from the heart, before he turned his back on them and disappeared among the other Moors inside the Medina. Gerard unlocked the car and Elinor got in hastily, tired from her long walk through the *souks*.

'I hadn't realised before how enormous the *souks* here are,' she murmured. 'They're much bigger than the ones at Meknes.'

'Much!' Gerard agreed. 'Terrible place for getting one-self lost, though. One could disappear there and never be heard of again!'

Elinor shivered and he put his hand over hers with an affectionate gesture.

'I am sorry,' he said. 'That was tactless of me!'

Elinor shook her head. 'Not really. It's silly of me to mind. I expect seeing Zachary again properly will make me feel differently. At the moment I can't really believe that he's still alive, let alone what it was like to be in love with him. It's as if I had married him in a dream and it has nothing to do with reality. Does that make sense to you?'

He put the car into gear and crept slowly out of the car park.

'It will take you time to get used to his being back,' he said gently. 'Perhaps you never were in love with him. Young girls often imagine themselves to be in love when they are no more than in love with love.'

Elinor sighed, relieved that he should understand so well.

'At the time I was fathoms deep in love with him!' she remembered. 'It's only now that I feel nothing at all!'

Gerard smiled.

'Good!' he said, and Elinor blushed. Gerard was nice and terribly easy to talk to, but a wise girl kept silent about such things, especially when the man she was talking to was the one her father had picked out to take good care of her future.

Walter Kendon was sitting in the patio watching the birds when they got home. He sat on the shady side, drinking a pressed lemon and studying a handful of papers which were balanced precariously on his lap. He half rose at his daughter's entrance, but as the papers threatened to slip from his grasp, he sat back again thankfully and smiled up at the two of them.

'You make a very handsome couple!' he told them.

Elinor patted him gently on the head. 'Shut up, Father,' she said with familiar disrespect. 'You'll embarrass Gerard if you go on like that!'

Gerard grinned at her. 'Not at all!' he insisted. 'I'm highly flattered. No one ever thinks I look handsome on my own!'

She was obliged to laugh.

'You're impossible, both of you!' she smiled at them.

'I'll leave you to talk about business, while I go and wash. The dust in the Medina in Fez is quite unbelievable!'

Her father grunted. 'Always was! Dreadful in the hot weather, of course. I never enjoyed my trips there much. It's different now that I have an able young assistant to do those jobs for me!'

Elinor was on the point of protesting, remembering how her father had exulted in the battle with the local tradesmen, no matter what he had set out to buy. But the pride in Gerard's eyes stopped her. He was plainly delighted that Mr. Kendon was so pleased with him. And why not? Elinor asked herself. She was glad that somebody could be made happy so easily.

The maid had closed the shutters in her room. She switched on the electric light, wondering as she did so why all people except the English always wanted to shut out the sun and the fresh air. She went over to the hand basin and turned on the tap, knowing from experience that it would be a minute or two before the water ran hot.

She had just begun to undress when she heard footsteps coming up the marble steps outside and a second later her father's manservant was knocking on the door.

'Yes?' she called out. 'What do you want?'

'Somebody wants to speak to you downstairs, *madame*!'

'On the telephone?'

'No, *madame*.'

'Then please tell my father. I'm changing.'

'He wishes to see you, *madame*. He asked me not to inform your father. I've put him in the *salon*.'

Elinor grunted and pulled her dress back on. She ran a swift comb through her hair and made a face at herself in the looking-glass, deciding that what make-up she had on would have to do.

The *salon* was almost as dark as her bedroom had been. Elinor stood in the doorway and tried to make out who it was that had got to his feet in the gloomy interior.

'Yes?' she said uncertainly.

'Hullo, wife!' said Zachary.

Elinor blushed and then she was angry.

'It seems to be entirely a relationship of convenience,' she snapped. 'Your convenience! After all, I suppose if you can acknowledge me only when you feel like it, I can do the same to you!'

Zachary looked at her long and hard.

'I can't remember ever denying the fact that you are my wife,' he said with a lack of interest that was nicely calculated to make her angrier than ever.

'No, you just disappeared for two years!' she retorted.

'That was hardly my fault,' he said mildly. 'However, I have no intention of forcing an explanation on you about that. I've come to ask you a favour.'

'Oh?' Elinor asked cautiously, her curiosity preventing her from turning him down out of hand.

He smiled at her with all the old magic.

'My cousin has arrived from Australia,' he explained cheerfully. 'It wouldn't be entirely *comme il faut* for her to come to my place, seeing that you aren't there, so I thought you might put her up here?'

Elinor gasped. '*Your* cousin?'

He smiled angelically at her. 'Well, your cousin too, I suppose, in a way. She's outside in the car.'

'Then she can stay there!' Elinor snapped.

But Zachary paid her no heed at all.

'It will do you good to meet your Australian family,' he said calmly. 'And I can't think of anyone better for you to begin with than Lillemor!'

Elinor glared at him, but that seemed to amuse him more than ever.

'I'll ask her in,' he said.

CHAPTER FIVE

ELINOR ran after him, clinging to his sleeve.

'Zachary! Don't do that! Tell me about her first, please. You know how difficult it is to persuade my father to accept anyone!'

He stopped obediently.

'He seems to have accepted that assistant of his gladly enough,' he said dryly.

'That's different!' Elinor said miserably. 'He found him for himself!'

Zachary stared at her. 'Oh? I thought he'd found him for you!'

Elinor's control on her temper receded a step further.

'What if he did? Where have you been all this time? I was much better off without you!'

The tension returned to Zachary's face. 'Indeed?' he said coldly. 'Then we shall have to see what can be done about it, won't we? In the meantime I'm bringing Lillemor in and you're going to look after her—nicely! She's come a long way to see me, and even if you can't understand it, she deserves a decent welcome. Is that understood?'

Elinor hesitated. 'Where have you been, Zachary?' she asked at last.

He walked deliberately towards the door.

'I'll tell you one day,' he promised, 'when you're really interested and not just sorry for yourself!'

Elinor stamped her foot. But it was too late. Zachary had already left the room. Impatiently, she opened the shutters and tried to make the room look a little more welcoming. Why did Zachary have to have female cousins anyway? If it had been a man, he could have looked after him himself. It wasn't at all easy to entertain strangers in her father's house. He would ask awkward questions and make snide remarks about Zachary's morals. Elinor sighed and thumped open the windows, marvelling at the soft, scented air that came in to greet her. It was such a pretty land, and yet it could be both dramatic and cruel. On this occasion, it seemed to her, she had been met with nothing but trouble. The thought of Zachary gnawed at her and yet she couldn't bring herself to acknowledge herself as his wife. It had all been such a ghastly error for him as much as for her. Perhaps one day she would gain her freedom and marry Gerard, with his pleasant ways and undemanding needs, and then she would be happy.

The laughter in the hall told that Zachary and his cousin were on very good terms indeed. Elinor frowned and went to the door to greet the Australian woman, curious to find out what she was like and what had brought her all the way from Australia in search of her cousin. At first sight she was terrifyingly beautiful, Elinor thought in almost a panic. But it was not really beauty, she noted. It was more the result of extremely careful grooming and wearing clothes that she knew were exactly suited to her. She was very fair, but her skin was finely tanned, and she wore the palest of lipsticks, so there was nothing that stood out much in her face, not even her blue eyes.

'Lillemor, I want you to meet Elinor. Elinor, my cousin Lillemor Wild.'

Elinor took a quick step forward and held out her hand.

'How d'you do?' she said quickly. Her hand was met by a limp clasp from the other girl.

'Zac said you might be on the formal side!' was all Lillemor said. 'Being brought up by that father of yours, an' all!'

'And all?' Elinor repeated sweetly.

Lillemor was completely unperturbed. 'I meant not knowing your mother,' she said calmly. 'It makes life that little bit harder, doesn't it?'

'I've never thought about it,' confessed Elinor. 'I can't even remember my mother, so I suppose I've never felt the lack of what I didn't know!'

Lillemor smiled graciously. 'How brave of you!' she said.

Elinor blinked and looked at Zachary for help, but he seemed to have none to offer her.

'I'd never thought of it that way!' he drawled. 'Perhaps you have never had an example of what married life should be. Very interesting!'

Elinor drew herself up.

'I told you,' she said in a voice that hovered on the edge of tears, 'that I don't consider myself married to you. It was all a mistake and it lasted for such a short time——'

'And your father didn't approve!' he added wickedly.

'That has nothing to do with it!' she snapped.

'Nothing?' he repeated, daring her to deny it again.

'Well, not much, anyway,' she added uncomfortably.

Lillemor looked on, amused. She gave a slight laugh which directed both of their attentions to her. Immediately she apologised for interrupting their quarrel.

'I hadn't realised how truly married you are!' she said silkily. 'Arguing the minute you set eyes on each other! Poor Zachary, I can see it will take you some time to get used to the idea that you've lost your sparring partner!'

Zachary looked annoyed. 'I haven't—yet!' he reminded them both.

'Never mind,' Lillemor ccmforted him, just as if he hadn't spoken at all, 'you can always quarrel with your family. I,' she added with a sparkle, 'should enjoy it very much, I have no doubt!'

'No doubt!' Elinor agreed dryly. She looked at the Australian girl with a renewed interest, a little shocked that she should be able to be jealous of her. She was so very much Zachary's type—suave and distinguished-looking and probably very witty. Other virtues, like loyalty and openness, were not the ones that Zachary looked for.

Zachary smiled and looked pleased with himself. Was it something she had said? Elinor wondered. She felt the back of her hands prickling with her annoyance and wished that she could think of something really crushing to say which would deal with both the Wilds once and for all, but nothing came to mind.

'Perhaps you'd like to come through to the patio, to meet my father?' she suggested to Elinor. 'Zachary had the guest room last night and I'll have to make sure that the servants have got it ready for you.'

'Okay,' Lillemor accepted lazily. 'I have a yen to meet this father, I must say!' Her eyes twinkled maliciously. 'I've heard so much about him, I can hardly believe him to be true!'

'Oh?' Elinor said in her best hostess voice. 'What have you heard?'

'Why, only that he's a cross of Mr. Barrett of Wimpole Street and some patriarch or other!'

Elinor cast a speaking look at Zachary, who only shrugged his shoulders and grinned.

'He is a bit awesome!' he put in cheerfully.

'Not when you get to know him!' Elinor retorted as crushingly as she could.

'Perhaps not,' he agreed amiably enough. 'But then I never really had the opportunity to get to know him, did I?'

'And whose fault was that?' Elinor demanded.

'Well, who can tell?' he asked. 'I suppose it was just circumstances. You'd better lead on and warn your father that we're coming. I gathered as I came in that he was talking business with that Frenchman of yours, and you know how he hates any business to get interrupted.'

Elinor did know, and the fact made it impossible for her to answer Zachary as she would have liked. Instead she contented herself with making as dignified an exit as she could. But her feet dragged as she walked through the house to the patio. Her father was not going to like having to play host to a relation of Zachary's and he would voice the fact only too clearly. Elinor was not sure that she liked Lillemor much herself, but that didn't mean that she wanted to make the girl feel uncomfortable—if she could feel uncomfortable, that was. She looked more than able to take care of herself in almost any circumstances. It was very odd that she should arrive so conveniently at that!

Walter Kendon looked up at his daughter with undoubted displeasure.

'Can't you see we're busy now?' he asked her testily.

'I'm sorry, Father,' she said meekly. 'I thought I ought to tell you that Zachary's cousin is going to stay with us for a while.'

'Zachary's what?' he exploded.

'His cousin,' Elinor repeated in even more timid tones.

'Good heavens! Has he got a cousin?' Mr. Kendon demanded. 'I'd never thought of him having any relations. Never had any to that stage wedding he had here!'

'They live in Australia,' Elinor explained patiently.

'Well, he can't stop here,' her father said with decision, and returned to the papers he held in his hand.

'But it isn't a he, it's a she,' Elinor explained. 'I've *said* she could stay!'

'Then you'd better keep her out of my way!' he replied. 'And out of Gerard's. The boy can't spend his whole time entertaining you and your friends, you know. He's got other things to do!' He remembered that on the contrary he was trying to promote a friendship between Gerard and his daughter and changed his mind. 'Not that I mind him hobnobbing with you, you understand,' he grunted. 'But not with this other girl. A cousin of Zachary's indeed! Shares the same bad blood, I shouldn't wonder!'

'Indeed I do!' Lillemor said from the entrance to the patio. 'All his worst characteristics come from my side of the family!'

Walter Kendon erupted to his feet, scattering papers all over the courtyard. Gerard and Elinor tried hurriedly to retrieve them and ended up by colliding with each other. Only Lillemor and Zachary made no effort to move at all.

'You sound very proud of the fact!' Mr. Kendon grunted at Lillemor. 'Not that I believe you for a minute. No one as pretty as you could possibly be like Zachary!' And he actually smiled.

Elinor looked on in amazement, reflecting that a really pretty girl could do almost anything with any man, and then chiding herself for being cynical. It should have been something in the nature of a relief that her father seemed prepared to like Lillemor as she was to stay in his house, and Elinor simply couldn't understand why she wasn't pleased at all. She looked angrily at Gerard, but he at least had no interest in the Australian girl. Instead he was gazing fondly at her. Silly sheep, she thought before she could stop herself, and by way of penance, she smiled extra warmly back at him and was moderately heartened by the way his eyes immediately shone with pleasure.

Mr. Kendon made his chair available for Lillemor, smiling more than Elinor had seen him do for years. Almost gaily, he clapped his hands and asked the servants to bring pressed lemon drinks for everyone and to see that the spare room was made ready for Miss Wild. Even the name of Wild didn't seem to disturb him unduly.

'When did you leave Australia?' he asked her.

Lillemor neatly crossed her long attractive legs and surveyed them with pleasure before replying.

'I was coming anyway,' she said. 'I decided to fly when the only answer I got to my letter to Zachary was some official communication from the Moroccan government. As it was in Arabic and French, I couldn't understand a word of it. I tried to get someone to translate it, but all they could tell me was that Zac was missing. I just didn't believe them, but I thought I'd better hurry myself to see what was going on. I didn't know about his being married then,' she added with faint malice.

Mr. Kendon brushed away her remark as calmly as he would have an annoying fly.

'That was all a bit of a mistake,' he said firmly. 'My daughter was too young to know what she was doing. She's come to see that it was doomed to failure, haven't you, Elinor?'

Elinor opened her mouth to agree with him, but no words would come. She was bitterly conscious of Zachary watching her every movement.

'Well?' her father prompted her.

'I suppose so,' she said unhappily.

'Well, that's good!' Lillemor openly rejoiced. 'My parents have always paired me off with Zac. They think we're two of a kind and might be able to control each other!' She smiled up at Mr. Kendon, deliberately flirting with him, but in such a delicate way that nobody could possibly have objected. 'Tell me, Mr. Kendon, do you think I should be able to control that cousin of mine?'

Mr. Kendon looked upset.

'Really, my dear, it's hardly my place to advise you—especially if your family have no objections, but your cousin is such a very unreliable young man!'

'He's a doctor!' Lillemor reminded him slyly.

'A doctor, yes! But not in a settled practice or anything like that. Not the sort of life for any young woman with children to bring up!'

Lillemor smiled lazily at her cousin. 'I can see you think he's cut out to be a bachelor all his days?' she drawled.

'Yes!' Mr. Kendon agreed enthusiastically. 'Most unreliable!'

Zachary burst out laughing. 'Aren't you overlooking one little thing?' he inquired.

Mr. Kendon's smile died. He rounded on Zachary, his

cheeks quivering with indignation.

'How could we ever forget?' he demanded hoarsely. 'If you were a gentleman, you wouldn't remind us!'

Elinor was more embarrassed than she could say. She wished she could say the first thing that came into her head with the elegant ease that Lillemor seemed to, but she couldn't. All she could do was tie herself up in emotional knots and hope that in the end somebody else would make the decision for her. She stole a glance at Zachary and was relieved to see that he, at least, didn't look at all annoyed. His thin, bony face was still set in the lines of laughter. He had taken off his coat and she couldn't help noticing how his bones stuck through his shirt, he had become so thin. What he needed was some proper feeding, she thought indignantly, and found herself blushing. If she were a proper wife, wouldn't she be doing the feeding? she thought with dismay.

'Zachary, why don't you stay on to dinner?' she asked him impulsively.

His eyes played over her face.

'It's a kind thought, Elinor,' he said gravely, 'but half measures won't do, you know.'

Elinor blushed again. 'You're looking thin,' she complained.

'I know,' he smiled. 'Skinny as a rake. When I get settled in my own house, I'll employ you to come and cook for me twice a week!'

'All right,' Elinor said bravely. The tears were beginning to burn at the back of her eyes and she was afraid she would disgrace herself entirely by crying over him, just as if he *meant* something to her! And she wouldn't do that! Because she couldn't make up her mind about him at all. If he would only offer an explanation of where he had been all this time and not expect her to take everything on trust. It wasn't fair!

'You'd better leave it to your cousin,' Lillemor advised

him, as if the whole matter was now settled. 'I'm just longing to see this house of yours. It'll give me no end of a kick to set up housekeeping for you! Where is this place?'

Zachary shrugged. 'This is the life!' he grinned. 'To have two women ready to do for me is my idea of bliss!'

'It won't be when we quarrel over your kitchen!' his cousin warned him, her voice warm and amused. 'You'd far better leave the whole thing to me!'

Zachary looked at Elinor, but she refused to play. She wasn't going to *beg* to be allowed to do his chores, she thought indignantly.

'Okay,' said Zachary. 'But it's in the old part of the town, in the poorest part. I don't know if you would care for it.'

Elinor's eyes shone with excitement.

'Right inside the Medina?' she asked. Her father's house was old too, but it was in a far more spacious district and they had mostly Europeans for neighbours. Right inside the Medina seemed much more exotic and foreign and one's neighbours would be Moorish and exciting.

'Yes, why not?' Zachary smiled at her. 'I like to live among my patients when I can.'

Only Mr. Kendon was able to find any objection to the location. Frank envy was written on all their faces.

'You'll get rats in the house!' Mr. Kendon grunted fiercely.

'Nonsense,' Zachary retorted. 'I'd like to see the Arabs tolerating rodents in their houses. They're exhaustingly clean! Washing blankets and carpets every week! Scrubbing all the furniture! And if I hadn't put a stop to it the floors would be awash with water morning, noon and night!'

Elinor giggled, remembering that their own servants were just the same and that there was nothing they liked better than to wash the marble floors of the long corridors, hating the dust that inevitably blew in through the windows

69

and door.

'I'd love to see you holding your surgery there!' she exclaimed.

He looked at her seriously. 'You're welcome any time,' he said gravely. 'You only have to say the word!' But Elinor wasn't sure what she would be saying the word to. To a visit would be lovely, but she didn't want to go in deeper than she was ready for.

'I'll come with Lillemor one day,' she said shyly.

'Right,' he agreed readily enough. It was impossible to tell if he was disappointed by her lack of response. 'I'll give her a plan of the district so that she can find me.'

Elinor bit her lip. She wanted to have the plan if anyone was going to have it, but she couldn't bring herself to ask him for it. Instead she sat up very straight and sipped her ice-cold lemon drink and wished that she was dead, or safely back in England, or at the very least back in the emotional cocoon she had wound for herself over the last two years.

It was flat after Zachary had gone. Elinor offered to take Lillemor to her room and spent a little while explaining to her the eccentricities of the plumbing, which had yards of lead piping apparently leading nowhere, but how it was absolutely fatal to disturb them.

'How comic!' Lillemor commented. 'I should have thought your father would have been a bit of a perfectionist in these matters.'

'He is,' Elinor answered. 'He was defeated by the plumber, though. He had even more firmly held ideas of his own!'

Lillemor looked sideways at the shower. 'Oh well,' she said, 'I guess you've managed all these years!'

Elinor laughed. 'It *does* work,' she insisted. 'In some ways that's the most annoying thing about it.'

Lillemor raised her eyebrows. 'I can see that!' she said.

Elinor left her guest to unpack and went down to the

patio to rejoin her father and Gerard. Her father was sitting in the very last of the sun. The lengthening rays gave him a ruddy look of good health which was not really there, but for a moment he looked young and hearty and Elinor smiled to think what a handsome man he had been in his day.

She sat down in one of the deck-chairs and stretched her legs out in front of her. They were not as good as Lillemor's, perhaps, but they were nice legs and she had no reason to be ashamed of them.

'It's been quite a day, hasn't it?' she said aloud.

Her father squinted at her through the sunset.

'Tired, darling?' he asked her.

She nodded. 'I wish Zachary would say where he's been all this time,' she said on a sigh. 'I'd so like to know that he couldn't help himself!'

'Of course he could help himself! I didn't tell you today, my dear, as you've only just come home yourself, but I rang up my solicitor this morning. He can't hold you to that marriage of yours. Not a chance of that! I've told my fellow to serve papers on him for a divorce, or an annulment, or whatever is best in the circumstances.'

Elinor sighed. 'I wish you'd waited,' she said.

'Wait for what?' her father demanded. 'You're a procrastinator by nature, Elinor. You'd never do anything at all!'

Elinor looked straight into the sun. It made her eyes hurt, but it was beautiful. A second later, it was no more than an enormous scarlet ball on the horizon.

'I'm not sure I believe in divorce,' she said.

Her father made an impatient gesture. 'It isn't divorce at all in my eyes!' he exclaimed angrily. 'It never was a proper marriage!'

Elinor looked at her father. 'It seemed it at the time,' she said.

'Nonsense! You were far too young to know what you

were doing! I said so at the time, but you wouldn't listen to me!'

'No,' Elinor admitted. It had all been such a breathless and exciting rush and she had been so very much in love. She had thought Zachary the sun, the moon and the stars!

'This fellow will do everything, Elinor,' her father said gruffly. 'You won't have to bother with it all. There's no need to be miserable about it!'

'No,' she said again. She sat in silence for a long minute. 'But I wish I knew what Zachary was going to say about it all,' she said at last. She was nervous of what he might do. Zachary, as she remembered him, was a man who was well capable of taking care of his own, and yet he had hardly spoken to her since he had come home, and surely a man who was still in love would do that?

Her father grunted. 'He won't say anything!' he said with contempt. 'He's got that cousin of his now!'

Lillemor managed to look quite beautiful when she came down to dinner. She had dressed her hair in a different way and wore sweet-smelling flowers in it, that added a fragrance to the air as she moved. Her dress was simple, but it was also formal and she could have worn it anywhere at all—perhaps she had in Australia, who knew?

She took her seat on Walter Kendon's right hand and smiled across the table at Gerard.

'Do you always eat here?' she asked him.

The Frenchman shook his head. 'I am not so fortunate!' he smiled. 'But I never refuse an invitation. Mr. Kendon has one of the best cooks in Meknes!'

Lillemor looked pleased. She watched with interest as the soup was brought in and sniffed it appreciatively.

'I can see the French influence is very strong,' she said, much gratified. 'How very nice!'

Walter Kendon, who took his meals almost as seriously as he took his business, smiled at her.

72

'The French were here for a long time,' he explained. 'One can see their influence in a lot of things. But Morocco remains very much itself all the same. As soon as you go out of the modern parts of the towns, or away from the main arteries that join the country together, you are back in Morocco as she must have been in the Middle Ages.'

Lillemor nodded her head and the scent of the flowers she wore spread through the patio.

'It sounds exciting,' she admitted. 'But I'm quite content where I am, getting the best of both worlds!'

Mr. Kendon looked satisfied. 'And a very charming guest you make, my dear!' he told her.

Elinor found herself eating the meal almost mechanically. She felt uneasy about her father's action in calling in his solicitor. Zachary would expect her to deal with the matter herself, she thought, and that added a twist to the gnawing anxiety she felt about the whole affair. She tried talking to Gerard, but there didn't seem to be much to say. In a half-hearted way, they discussed her father's business and the variety of objects that they now made for sale. Gerard had plans of his own for expanding their trade.

'There's no reason why we should confine ourselves to leather goods,' he remarked with enthusiasm. 'I can see us exporting carpets, camel blankets—everything! Why not? All the local goods would be immensely popular all over Europe.'

Elinor tried desperately not to yawn. The harder she tried, the more the urge strove to master her. It was something of a relief when the meal came to an end and her father decided to show Lillemor his garden by moonlight. It was a romantic sight, Elinor had to admit, when some of the most sweet-smelling of the flowers opened themselves up to greet the moon, but she was too tired to want to go with them. She barely noticed that Gerard stayed behind too.

'Your father tells me you're going to be free of Zachary,'

he broke into her thoughts. He sounded nervous and excited.

'I suppose so,' Elinor replied. 'There doesn't seem to be anything else to do, does there?'

Gerard came over and stood by her chair. 'Remember what I told you when I first saw you?' he asked her.

Elinor sat up straight in a rush. 'Not now, Gerard,' she begged him.

But she was too late, for, leaning down, Gerard kissed her on the lips, lightly, almost experimentally at first, but then he gathered her into his arms and kissed her again. It was nice to be kissed, to be needed again, and Elinor clung to him. But her second thought told her that this was not at all the same as the kisses she had shared with Zachary.

CHAPTER SIX

ELINOR cried herself to sleep that night. Once she had started she couldn't stop. She buried her face in the pillow and cried and cried. Funnily enough she felt better when it was all over, and by morning she felt quite herself again and far less tense and worried. Everything, she told herself, would eventually work out and all she had to do was to wait until they did, getting hurt as little as possible and trying not to hurt too many other people.

The maid brought her her early morning tea just as the dawn was breaking in the sky. Outside she could hear the faithful being called to prayer from the nearby mosque, the Arabic phrases coming clearly through the light morning breeze.

'Monsieur Roche wondered if you would join him for breakfast in half an hour,' the maid told her, her voice rigid with disapproval.

'Here?' Elinor asked in surprise. She knew that Gerard had 'digs' somewhere in Meknes and had not expected him to be calling so early.

'In the patio,' the maid said sourly.

Elinor thought about it for a moment.

'What's my father doing?' she asked at last.

'He is tired. He will have his breakfast in his room. These days he becomes tired very easily.'

Elinor knew a moment of sharp anxiety. Was there anything wrong with her father? she wondered. He looked so much older than when she had seen him last, and then he certainly wouldn't have needed to rest in the early morning. He would keep it from her for as long as he could if anything were the matter, she thought. Perhaps that was why he was so anxious to get her future settled in the way he wanted. She would ask him at the first opportunity, putting on her best professional air and hoping to get an honest answer.

'Is there anything wrong with him?' she asked the maid.

'There could be,' the maid responded. 'He missed you more than he would admit while you were in England. Why don't you ask him?'

'I think I will,' Elinor said with determination. 'And I'll wring an answer out of him too!'

The maid smiled. 'And what shall I say to Monsieur Roche?' she asked.

Elinor frowned. 'Tell him I'm just coming,' she said.

Gerard was reading the paper when she went down to the patio. He stood up immediately and held her chair for her to sit down at the table beside him.

'I wanted to see you,' he began with a smile.

'Yes?' Elinor prompted him.

He shrugged his shoulders. 'I just wanted to see you!' he admitted. 'I wanted to talk about what happened last night—if you don't mind, that is?' he added with solicitude.

'And if I do?' she asked lightly.

Gerard flushed. 'I-I was hoping that you felt about it as I did,' he began awkwardly.

Elinor's eyes crinkled with amusement. 'I've forgotten all about it!' she said. 'If that's what you want?'

'No, oh no!' he protested. 'I-I liked it! I mean, I really wanted to kiss you——' He broke off helplessly. 'I'm making a ghastly hash of this,' he said. 'What I want to say is this. I wanted to kiss you. I want to kiss you now! But I have to remember that you are still married to *him*, don't I?'

Elinor still looked amused. 'We both do,' she agreed.

Gerard looked suddenly eager. 'Do you mean that you were on the point of forgetting last night?' he asked hopefully.

Elinor hesitated. It didn't seem kind to give him hope that she was far from feeling herself.

'My marriage was so long ago,' she tried to explain. 'We had a fortnight together before Zachary went, and we had had very little longer in which to get to know each other before that. Sometimes it seems no more than a romantic dream! He seems to be a stranger to me. Can you understand that?'

Gerard nodded gravely.

'But it will come right in the end, won't it? You'll be free of him one day and then you can marry me!'

Elinor bit her lip. 'But in the meantime I'm married to him,' she said flatly. 'And I'm not sure that I believe in divorce, or anything like that.'

'Your father says you can have the wedding annulled!' Gerard protested immediately.

Elinor sighed. 'He says so,' she said. 'But I don't see how. I don't know what the law is. Legally, last time I inquired, I was a widow. I can hardly still be that with a husband still living, can I?'

Gerard considered. 'I should think the courts would take all the facts into consideration,' he said at last.

'Then you're a great deal more hopeful than I am!' Elinor retorted. 'Think of all the war brides in the past who hardly knew their husbands—and other people like that!'

Gerard made a Gallic gesture with his hands.

'But there has been no war, *petite*,' he objected. 'It was not his country which took Zachary away from you.'

'No,' said Elinor with considerable feeling. 'It was not!'

'Well then, we have reason to be cheerful!' the Frenchman decided. 'I fancy your father will find some way out of the difficulty for you!'

Elinor frowned. 'That's what I keep telling myself,' she said. 'But Zachary hasn't said what he wants yet. He isn't the sort of person one can lightly push to one side if he doesn't want to be pushed. I can't help thinking it would be

77

wiser to wait until he says what he's going to do.'

Gerard looked amused and slightly contemptuous.

'Your father could break his thin body between his two fingers!' he sneered. 'Leave it to him.'

But Elinor shook her head. 'You don't know Zachary!' she warned him gently. 'You don't know Zachary at all!'

Gerard's eyebrows slid upwards, but he said nothing at all. It was plain enough that he didn't believe her.

It was pleasant having their breakfast on the patio. The birds, newly woken, were in full voice and it was still too early to be hot. Elinor drank her coffee with real pleasure, rejoicing in the newly-baked rolls and the fresh butter that was so different from the food she had become accustomed to in the nurses' home in London.

'I suppose I should have asked Lillemor to share this with us,' Elinor said after a long silence. 'It seems rather a shame to deprive her of the early morning.'

Gerard bit into his roll and jam with gusto.

'I shouldn't worry about her! She strikes me as the type who can very well look after herself. I don't suppose she rises before noon and when she does rise she will have everybody tripping over themselves to make her comfortable! I don't think you need bother yourself!'

He was not so very far out in his prophecy. By eleven o'clock, Elinor had given up her guest and was beginning to think what she wanted to do herself. She had taken a book into the patio after breakfast, but she didn't want to spend the whole day reading and, on the other hand, she had thought that she ought to be available when Lillemor did finally come down stairs.

She was still considering the problem when her father's manservant brought Zachary out to join her. Elinor was completely unprepared for him and she could feel herself blushing as she slowly rose to greet him, and that made her angry, which made her blush all the more.

'Where is everybody?' he asked her with indifference.

Elinor looked away from his piercing eyes, afraid of what they would see.

'They're not up yet,' she said. 'Zachary, I wish you'd look at my father some time. I'm sure he's not well.'

'Not very, I should think,' Zachary replied gently. 'But nothing much to worry about. I should think he suffers from high blood pressure and isn't doing anything about it. Getting so excited about everything won't be doing him any good, you know.'

Elinor sat down again. 'I know. But there's nothing I can do about it, is there?'

His eyes mocked her. 'A great deal, I should say. He has no need to be so concerned about you, has he? You may be his only daughter——'

'You may as well go on and say it!' Elinor said angrily as he broke off.

'Possibly. It needs saying by someone,' he agreed calmly. 'You may be his daughter, but you are also a married woman!'

Elinor looked up at him resentfully. 'I don't feel like one!' she complained.

He grinned. 'You did at one time!' he teased her. 'And don't deny it, because *I* shouldn't believe you!'

'It wouldn't be so bad now if you would only say where you'd been all this time!' she complained. 'I don't think I'm asking too much in that!'

He bent over, brushing her cheek with his fingers.

'You could have a little faith in me,' he suggested, almost sadly.

'Two years!' she retorted.

Zachary stood up straight again, looking disappointed.

'Never mind. Forget that I asked! Suppose we forget that we once, in an ill-considered moment, married each other and take it from there? We can pretend that we've only just met and that we're strangers with everything to learn about one another.'

79

'So we are!' Elinor put in.

He turned on her, looking really angry for the first time.

'Are we? I suppose that's why I know that you take your bath too hot and that you sleep on your tummy! I know other things about you too, but I expect you would rather that I didn't enumerate them here and now!'

'Yes, I should!' Elinor admitted hastily. 'All right, I'll pretend that we've just met, if you will?'

With that sudden change of mood that had always attracted her, he smiled at her.

'Well,' he said, 'if I've only just met you, perhaps I'll invite you out to something! What would you like?'

Her own spirits lifted as if by magic.

'I want to know where you live,' she said frankly.

He laughed. 'Your wish is my command! I'll come and collect you this evening and you can cook my dinner for me!'

A small whirlwind of excitement rose in Elinor's middle.

'But what about Lillemor?' she objected.

Zachary considered the problem.

'I suppose, seeing I've just met you, you ought to have a chaperone of some sort,' he said.

Elinor frowned. 'You mean you'll ask her too?' she said flatly. It wouldn't be the same thing at all with his cousin there!

'Unless you particularly ask me not to,' he answered. 'I'm prepared to have you on your own, if you like?'

'It would be very ill-mannered not to include her!' Elinor remarked earnestly.

'Very!' he agreed.

She hesitated, gathering her courage together. Finally she burst out:

'I'd very much rather she wasn't there!'

Zachary looked unbearably pleased with himself.

'Then I'll make some excuse to her,' he said, apparently having no doubts that he could manage Lillemor as easily as he had managed Elinor. 'She can come some other time on her own and then it will be fair!'

It was, of course, quite impossible to say that this wasn't what she wanted either. Elinor glared down at her hands in her lap and wondered at the prickle of resentment that was slowly growing whenever she thought of Lillemor.

'How long is she staying?' she asked at last.

'Lillemor? Maybe six months. Knowing how our family is, she won't move before she's seen everything there is to see. She and I have always got along well together. I suppose that's why she thought she'd come and pay Morocco a visit!'

Elinor wished she knew what he was thinking. It was impossible to tell from his enigmatic eyes, and the slight swagger to his walk only told her that he was pleased with himself.

'What time shall I be ready?' she asked him, cross with herself that though she knew she was being manoeuvred she still wanted to go and see where he lived.

'I'll call for you at six o'clock,' he promised. 'And you'd better dress up, because I want to introduce you to some of my neighbours. Okay?'

'Okay,' she said, because after all, whenever Lillemor was asked to visit him, it was she who was going today.

Lillemor made no objection at all to her hostess going out for the evening with her cousin. She even offered to help her get ready.

'Zac tells me you're dressing up. Do you want any help? He said something about sending across a corsage for your dress.'

'Zachary did?' Elinor said in complete disbelief.

Lillemor laughed wryly. 'We come from Australia, honey,' she said softly, 'but we're quite civilized really!'

Elinor was immediately contrite.

'Oh, I didn't mean that at all! Only for Zachary to be

81

doing such a thing! He doesn't usually play the gallant, does he?'

Lillemor's eyes narrowed, but she still smiled in the same pleasant way.

'Oh, I don't know,' she said. 'He has his little tricks, like everyone else, to keep the girls interested. He's always liked to stir up my jealousy.'

Elinor, who was not usually naïve, looked puzzled.

'But why?' she said at last.

Lillemor laughed.

'I've been in love with Zac ever since I can remember. He knows it too, the brute! It would be different if he was really married to you, of course, but we all know he isn't. This is my chance and I'm taking it. He knows that too.' She laughed. 'I can't see Zachary making himself an easy quarry, can you?'

'No,' said Elinor slowly, 'I can't.' She felt suddenly cold inside and frightened, though she knew not of what. 'How silly we are!' she added with determined gaiety. 'I must go and dress.'

She refused all further offers of help that Lillemor made her. She wanted to dress for Zachary by herself. She chose an evening dress of midnight blue. It was one she had left behind in Morocco when she had gone to England, but she didn't think that Zachary had ever seen it. It was shot through with silver and was elegant as well as being comfortable and easy to wear. Over it, hung loosely around her shoulders, she wore a locally made shawl, as light as gossamer and as white as snow. She thought she looked very well, with her silver slippers and silver chain handbag that held nothing at all but was pretty none the less. Aïlla was delighted with Zachary's corsage, even more so than Elinor. She brought it carefully, barely concealing her feeling of triumph.

'He has sent you pink roses!' she told Elinor. And there they were, the most delicately shaded pink rosebuds, stripped of their thorns, and bearing a card carrying the one letter Z.

'*Pink roses!*' the maid insisted. 'The flowers of love!'

'Zachary wouldn't know that!' Elinor retorted sharply.

But Aïlla only smiled to herself, quite sure in her own mind that Dr. Wild would certainly know all about the language of flowers. She pinned the corsage to Elinor's dress with care, her black eyes snapping with her own confident amusement.

'He'll soon show you that he is your husband when he has you alone tonight!' she told Elinor. 'You see if I'm not right!'

Elinor didn't reply immediately. What could she say? She could hardly explain to her maid that she and her husband had decided they had only just met. That they were strangers passing the time of day together. Nor could she tell her that Lillemor wanted Zachary and that that was why she had come from Australia. And she hadn't meekly given in to the official pronouncements of Zachary's death. She had believed in him enough to come thousands of miles to find him, to marry him and to live happily ever after.

These thoughts, which should not have disturbed her at all, gave Elinor a jumpy feeling. She went downstairs to wait for Zachary, wishing that she had refused his invitation. It would be much better for both of them if the break was a clean one, she thought. But that thought only made her lips tremble and the pervasive perfume of the roses was no help at all when it came to pulling herself together. She was a poor wife and a poor woman, she thought dismally. It was more than probable that even if she had welcomed Zachary with open arms, he wouldn't have wanted her. She would go back to London and she would nurse the sick and the aged, and that would be her life until she died!

She didn't want to go to the patio to join the others, so

83

she was glad when Zachary arrived a few minutes early and went to the door herself to greet him.

'Will you come in?' she asked him in forbidding tones.

His eyebrows shot up.

'I gather you would rather I didn't?'

Elinor blushed. 'Not exactly,' she compromised. 'Only I don't want to stir my father up again.' She wondered even as the words came tumbling out why she should involve her father in this. It was barely honest, she told herself, mildly shocked at her own subconscious inventiveness.

'All right,' Zachary drawled. 'Let's go!' He took her by the hand and pulled her out into the street, slamming the door behind him. It was not yet dark, in fact the business people were only beginning to go home, many of them dressed in *djellabahs* and their women in *haiks* and closely veiled. As they walked along the street, the men were careful not to stare at Elinor's naked face, the more polite pretending that they couldn't see her at all.

'Where *do* you live?' Elinor pressed Zachary, her curiosity getting the better of her.

'You'll see!' he said. He led the way through the Medina, nodding and smiling a greeting to various passers-by as he recognised them as ex-patients, or relatives of patients, most of whom would come with their sick relative, cluttering up his surgery with noisy sympathy for the sufferer. It was rare indeed for an ill person to come alone.

'It's a pretty noisy house,' he warned her. 'Do you think you'd like to live around here?'

Elinor considered the narrow alleyways, lit at night by a single naked electric light bulb, hung precariously at the intersections, mostly only serving to accentuate the surrounding black darkness. There was the indefinable smell of Arab cooking and charcoal that lingered on the streets as well, a pleasing aromatic mixture that was strange to her Western nose after her years in England. She was suddenly glad that it was not yet dark and that the huddled shapes

84

that made their way past her were still recognisable as human beings, knowing how ghostly their white figures could be at night.

'I think I would,' she said. 'Once I'd got used to it. Do you have your surgery here too?'

Zachary grinned. 'How polite you are!' he teased her. 'You don't have to make conversation with me!'

She winced. 'I don't understand!' she sighed. 'You're determined not to make things easier for me, aren't you?'

'No, I wouldn't say that,' he answered.

'But how did you get this house? You were away for two years, apparently dead, and yet you come home and immediately you're at home in a house, with a practice and everything you want——'

'Not everything!' he interrupted her. 'But I'm working on it!'

'There's still the house,' she said, and something of the hurt she was feeling showed in her voice.

He was immediately contrite. 'All right,' he said, 'I'll tell you about the house. I bought it when I first met you. I thought it would make a pleasant setting for my wife!' The dry tinge to his voice made her blush.

'You never told me anything about it!' she objected.

'It was going to be a surprise for you after our honeymoon. Only it didn't work out quite as I'd planned. But as I'd paid for the house, the previous owner kept it in good repair for me. It was here waiting for me when I came to inquire about it. A good thing too on the whole!'

Elinor flushed uncomfortably again.

'And your practice? I suppose that was just waiting for you as well?'

He nodded gravely.

'News gets around on the local grapevine much quicker than the official sources of information. They all knew I was coming—they probably knew it before I did!'

They had certainly known before she had. Elinor told

herself. She wondered if he had really bought the house for her and what it would be like.

'Where were you, Zachary?' she asked softly.

He shrugged his thin shoulders.

'Does it matter? We're strangers, don't forget! Your father,' he added, 'doesn't care where I've been, so why should you? I thought you'd both decided that it was all my own fault anyway.'

'How can we do otherwise unless you give us some explanation?' she cried out.

He looked completely indifferent.

'I think that's a question you have to answer for yourself,' he said.

They walked the last few yards in silence, until they came to a door that opened directly from the street in an otherwise completely solid wall. There were no windows, or any other outward sign that this was a habitation. There was only the door and the top leaves of a tree that trailed over the wall having grown too tall to be contained in the garden beyond.

'Is this it?' Elinor asked.

Zachary smiled and nodded.

'Shut your eyes and I'll open the door.' She did as she was bidden, a slight smile playing on her lips. She knew that now they were in the very poorest part of Meknes and she was almost sure that the house would be in keeping with its surroundings.

'All right,' said Zachary. 'You can open your eyes now!' He sounded almost unbearably pleased with himself and Elinor was more sure than ever that the whole thing was some kind of a joke.

'It is habitable?' she asked jokingly, but there was a note of seriousness beneath the question and his quick ears spotted it at once.

'Why don't you take a look?' he suggested, and there was no mistaking the disappointment that he was feeling. But why? she wondered. Did he expect her to take everything he did on trust?

She opened her eyes almost timidly and felt as though she had fallen into fairyland. She had never seen anything so beautiful, so magical as the house that Zachary had prepared for her. It was a feminine house, if such a thing is possible. It had none of the pretensions of her father's house. It was quite plain for the most part, with only the occasional piece of moulding round the ceilings and down the beautifully proportioned pillars that supported the roof. It was a small house, built round a courtyard to hide the life of the inhabitants from the prying eyes of outsiders. There was a receiving room for the men, where the husband could greet his friends, with its own separate door to the street, and another room for the women to sit and entertain. There were three bedrooms of varying sizes and, best of all, there was a fountain playing in the minute formal garden that grew oranges and peaches and a mass of flowers in boxes and precarious holes in the walls.

'It's beautiful!' she exclaimed.

'Well,' Zachary drawled, 'I'd figured that you'd become accustomed to beauty, living in your father's house. This isn't on the same scale, of course, but it has some charm.'

'Some charm!' she repeated angrily, put out that he should criticise this house which was everything she had ever dreamed of finding, even in Morocco, a country of magnificent dwellings.

'So you like it?' Zachary said, and he grinned at her. 'I rather thought you would!'

'Of course I do!' she exclaimed. 'You could use the man's sitting room as your surgery as it has an outside door of its own, couldn't you?' She hurried forward to take a closer look at some of the flowers in the small garden. 'I think it's absolutely beautiful!'

Zachary's face regarded her thoughtfully. With the shadows of the evening accentuating the hollows in his cheeks, she was made doubly aware of how terribly thin he was.

'I think it's rather nice too,' he said. 'I was terribly relieved to know that it had been kept for me—that it hadn't been sold again.' He paused, a curious, almost malicious look in his eyes. 'What do you think Lillemor is going to think of it?' he asked.

CHAPTER SEVEN

THE fact that Zachary's house was a genuinely Moorish one, completely unadapted to Western ideas of comfort, was made even more obvious at dinner. There were one or two divans, stuffed apparently with bricks and rags, and a few cushions should one wish to sit on the floor. The carpets on the other hand were superb as one might expect. The Moroccan has an enormous respect for the evil qualities that come from the ground and, if they can help it, their bare feet will never touch the earth at all. Even a dog must be fed on a plate or mat so that the goodness from the food will not be swallowed up in the contact with the earth. They cover their floors with carpets, their mosques with mats, and at weddings they carry their bride to ensure that her foot never touches the ground. Even on their visits to their mosques, they prefer to carry their prayer carpets with them as additional safeguard to the mats provided.

Zachary's house had carpets that would have graced a museum. They had all been hand-made of magnificent patterns and design, and were comfortable to stockinged feet that would have left their outdoor shoes at the entrance. Zachary himself had a pair of *babouches*, the Moorish long-toed slipper, which he wore with an air that secretly amused Elinor. She had expected to find him at home in his surroundings, but she had not expected that he would be more at home in Moorish dress than in what she had normally seen him in. He changed early on in the evening into a single loose garment that fell from his shoulders to the floor and looked quite indistinguishable from any other Arab as he sat on the floor on the other side of the brazier and lazily watched her as she cooked their meal.

A servant had lit the small charcoal stove out in the

street, blowing it from a single spark into a glowing coal with a specially made fan while she sat and gossiped with the neighbours. Once it was really going, she had brought it into the house and had set it down in the pretty little interior garden for Elinor to cook the meal. There were only the basic ingredients for the traditional *couscous*, with fresh fruit to follow, and Elinor was relieved that nothing more complicated was being asked of her, as she had never used such a primitive stove before and was beginning to think longingly of the enormous electric cooker her father had had installed in his house as a matter of course.

'Lillemor will feel at home with that thing,' Zachary said with a laugh. 'She always was good at picnics and things like that.'

Elinor, wrestling with a blunt knife and an unnamed lump of meat, glowered at him.

'Perhaps you should have asked her to come too after all!' she said bitterly.

Zachary leaned back on one elbow and looked pleased with himself.

'Why? I expect you'll manage to feed me somehow!' he said audaciously.

Elinor resisted the desire to throw the meat at his head.

'And is that all you were thinking of when you asked me?' she asked him, dangerously sweet.

He surveyed his thin body, not entirely without satisfaction.

'Well,' he excused himself, 'I think you'll agree that I do need feeding up!'

There was no doubt about that. It worried Elinor to see him quite so thin and with so many bones showing.

'I think you must have worms,' she muttered, hoping to shock him. But he only grinned at her.

'Very likely! Have you got a good cure for that too?'

She shied away from the idea of trying to cure him of anything.

'You forget,' she said with dignity, 'you're the doctor, I'm only a common or garden nurse!'

'Hmm, I'd forgotten that. It seems hard to think of you as being properly qualified now.' He looked at her with renewed interest. 'What are you going to do with your skills?'

Triumphantly, she succeeded in severing the meat and threw it into a pan. The *couscous* was already in a kind of double saucepan, the top one having holes in it like a sieve, and was steaming away.

'I don't know yet,' she answered him. 'I haven't had time to think. I'd like to be of some use here, but I don't know.'

'I see,' he said slowly. 'I suppose you want to be with your father?'

She nodded. 'I don't think he's well,' she said abruptly.

'No,' he agreed. 'Would you like to come and work for me?'

Elinor was so long answering him that he stopped lounging on his cushion and sat up straight, peering over the hot coals to see what she was thinking.

'Well?' he prompted her.

'Would you find it embarrassing?' she asked at last, biting her lip to hide her own distracted thoughts.

'I never find anything embarrassing!' he retorted smoothly. 'You forget, we're strangers who've only just met! I didn't even know that you are a fully qualified nurse, did I?'

'But it wouldn't be true, would it?' she said rather desperately. 'It would be there all the time!'

He lay back against his cushion again, his eyes alight with laughter.

'It will always be *there*, as you put it,' he said. 'It really happened to us. You can't escape that.'

'N-no,' she agreed. 'But it might be awkward all round!'

'I suppose you mean with young Gerard Roche! Why don't you say so?'

'No more than it would be for you with Lillemor!' she

exclaimed angrily, and then promptly wished she hadn't. She didn't want him to know that she was jealous of his Australian cousin—in any way at all!

'Oh, Lillemor is a practical soul,' he drawled. 'She would be able to see at a single glance that one can hardly exchange kisses with a hypodermic syringe in one's hand!'

'Oh, you think so?' Elinor jeered at him.

He deliberately yawned.

'Sure. I suppose you can't say the same for Roche. He looks the possessive Latin type to me!'

Elinor thought of Gerard's attachment to business and her father's wishes and found that she couldn't agree with him. There was nothing essentially romantic about Gerard that she could see. He was nice and she liked him. He was steady and she would always know exactly where she was with him, but he would never make her want to dance and sing as Zachary once had.

'All right,' she said deliberately. 'I'll work for you, if you want me to. But I shall expect my full rates of pay! I'm not going to work for nothing!'

'Not even for love!' he teased her. His tone changed to one of displeased earnestness. 'I'll pay you, Elinor. I'm not exactly a pauper, you know, and I do have a practice here.'

Elinor eyed him suspiciously. 'I don't suppose you get paid European rates, though?' she said.

'I don't,' he agreed simply. 'Sometimes I don't get paid at all. Sometimes I get paid a small fortune. But somehow I can't bring myself to see medicine, especially when it's needed as badly as it is here, as a business. I didn't think you would either.'

Elinor sighed, aware that he was disappointed in her.

'It isn't that,' she protested, aware that almost any explanation would sound rather feeble. 'Only I don't want to half do a job. If I wasn't being paid properly it would be difficult to go out when it was inconvenient at home. You know it would be!'

'I see,' Zachary said sadly. 'Another sop to your father!'

Elinor didn't answer him. She supposed it was true, though she didn't like to put it in quite such blunt terms. She sliced a green and a red pepper, cleaning out the centre and adding the sliced-up exteriors to the meat and vegetables cooking in the pan. An aromatic smell wafted up to meet her and she began to feel hungry. She turned the steaming *couscous* over with a spoon to make quite sure that it was cooking right through. They called it semolina in every Arabic glossary she had seen, and yet it didn't look like semolina. It had far more the consistency of millet. Whatever it was, though, it was good. She liked it quite as well as rice and more than a great many other things.

The blare of a native band warming up outside could just be heard in the garden. Drums and wailing horns were the favourites with an occasional crescendo caused by the firing of blunderbusses to add spice and real danger to the beat. This music had a distinctly Negro throb to it and Elinor found herself swaying in time to the drums. They must be quite close, she thought, for them to be able to hear them so distinctly.

Zachary bounced to his feet so suddenly that he startled her.

'You can begin work tomorrow!' he said with decision. 'Is that all right?'

Elinor nodded, glad that they were not going to discuss it any further.

'Quite all right,' she agreed with dignity. 'I'll be here.'

He looked down at her, his long robe flowing from his shoulders to his ankles. He looked foreign and incomprehensible—a stranger she had never even met. She was almost afraid of him, he looked so strange.

'Good,' he said.

Elinor listened to the music in silence, until that too came to an end, before beginning again with a lost primitive wail.

'Who are they?' she asked Zachary.

He smiled. 'Do you want to see? We could go when we've eaten. They're a Negro band, probably they are the descendants of slaves who were brought here. They have their own music and their own voodoo, like their cousins in the West Indies. They're quite famous, but it's not often that Europeans can see them. Mostly they perform at weddings and funerals, but they're quite respectable and tame then.'

'But not when they're on their own?' Elinor inquired.

Zachary grinned. 'Let's say they're different,' he said. 'They're a bit like the whirling dervishes of Persia. They roll themselves over red-hot coals and don't seem to feel a thing.'

'And they do that here in Meknes?' Elinor asked, astonished. She had lived in the city for the greater part of her life and she had never heard of any such thing.

Zachary's eyes mocked her.

'I can see you're going to learn a lot about Morocco working for me,' he said. 'Never mind, most of your ideas could do with a good shake-up!'

'What do you mean?' Elinor asked indignantly.

But he only looked even more amused.

'You'll find out!' he promised her. 'How long is that food going to be?'

'We can eat now,' she said reluctantly. 'Zachary, do you like me at all?' It wasn't what she had wanted to say, but the question had lain between them for so long and sooner or later she would have had to ask it, because she couldn't go on not knowing. She *had* to know!

'Do I like you?' he repeated. His teeth shone white in the light from the fire, adding to the malicious sparkle in his eyes. 'Now that's quite a question. I think I should require notice before I answer it. Do I like you?' he wondered aloud. 'I suppose I do.'

It wasn't exactly enthusiastic, Elinor thought, and swallowed in case her emotions should run away with her.

'I can't think why you married me if you only *suppose* so!' she exclaimed.

His eyes fastened on hers. 'Suppose you tell me why you married me?' he pressed her.

'I was in love with you,' she muttered.

'And did you like me as well?' he insisted.

'Of course I did!' She hesitated. 'I don't know. I didn't really know you at all, did I?'

'Not very well, perhaps,' he said gently. He sat down again and scooped the steamed *couscous* into an earthenware bowl, arranging the meat and vegetables on the top, while she sat and looked on. 'You worry too much,' he told her. 'I can wait, you know.'

'Wait for what?' she asked, puzzled.

He laughed. 'For the moon and the stars!' he teased her. 'What did you think?'

But Elinor wasn't prepared to confess what she had thought. She only knew that that let-down, smothered feeling was becoming almost commonplace in Zachary's company. If she wasn't very careful she would fall in love with him all over again. And then where would she be? He was only waiting to be free of her to go straight to his cousin! He had almost said so!

'You'd better eat a lot,' she said practically, 'and get some flesh on those bones!'

Zachary piled his plate high with every sign of intense satisfaction.

'I intend to!' he said.

'Balak! Balak!'

Elinor automatically moved out of the way of the man with his laden donkey who was trying to get past.

'Where on earth are they going at this time of night?' she remarked to Zachary.

'Same place as we are, I expect,' he answered her.

'They've probably heard that the devil dancers from Tetuan are here too!'

'Devil dancers!' Elinor scoffed. 'You wouldn't take me if they really were, would you?'

Zachary grinned in the darkness. He had a tight grip on her elbow which she had to admit she liked, and she was enjoying their slow walk towards the little square where the wail of music was coming from.

'I might,' he said.

But she didn't really believe him. True, the music was getting wilder and wilder, but then so was the hour getting later, and that was the way with all home-made music even in the West. She began to hurry in time with the beat and the rushing, padded feet all round her.

The *rhaïta*, the wailing oboe that sounded like bagpipes gone wild, began a slow intricate solo. At intervals the drums would accentuate the lonely, weird cry of the single instrument, wailing like a banshee at the crescent moon. There were a few human gasps of admiration and satisfaction and then the drums started to beat in earnest again. At the same moment Elinor and Zachary arrived at the square.

There was a single carpet of fire in the centre of the square. It had been burning brightly for several hours and now there was a good solid bed of coals that were red hot and would go on burning late into the night. There was very little flame, but then the fire was too hot for that now, it was a silent, throbbing, scarlet glow. Gathered around it were the spectators, their eyes bright with the reflection of the fire and their faces half hidden in the hoods of their *djellabahs* as if they were defying recognition. Elinor turned questioningly to Zachary and was surprised to notice that he was quite indistinguishable from his neighbours. Only she seemed to be in Western dress, but nobody appeared to mind. They moved apart to let her though, grunting in Arabic, or one of half a dozen dialects of Berber, as they wondered who she was and why she had come among them.

The devil dancers appeared not to notice the onlookers at all. Their leader could have been an Arab rather than a Negro, his skin was so pale and his features so sharp, but the dancers themselves were all shades of brown. Long ago their ancestors had been brought unwillingly north to serve as slaves, and these men, their descendants, were the result, as much Moroccans as any other citizen and yet still bearing the marks of their sad history. Mostly they performed at local weddings or funerals, but occasionally, for themselves, they would go through the whole of the ritual that had been handed down to them from their parents, calling on the Red Devil, the Devil of healing, the White Devil, who was female and who preferred to deal with her own sex, and all the other colours, Black, Blue and Yellow, who each had their own special place in their beliefs and who had somehow got tacked on to a belief in the One God, Allah, and Mohammed who is his prophet.

The players raised their *gargabous* high above their heads as they waited for their leader to nod out the new beat. Immediately the *rhaïta* was silent too and then, with a sudden crash, they all came to life again and the hot soul of Africa was poured forth in their melody.

'Why are they here?' Elinor asked Zachary.

'They're visiting. Probably their own relatives have asked them to come. Usually they stick pretty close to their home ground. Wait for it! Now watch!'

The dancers whirled in frenzied movements, hypnotising themselves into a complete trance. Their eyes began to stare and it was obvious they could neither see nor hear anything that was going on around them. Then, slowly, one by one, they approached the bed of coals and walked through it on their naked feet. Apparently they did not feel a single thing.

They whirled on, leaping to greater and greater heights.

97

The music throbbed with sound and rhythm until it was almost unbearable. The dancers moved round and round the fire. They were now in a deep trance and were more like sleepwalkers than wakeful men. The first one came to the fire, lay down beside it and rolled himself over the coals. He was followed by the others until they had all completed this remarkable feat. Once again the sobs of anxiety could be heard from the audience and then the music changed its beat and the dancers were ordinary men again, laughing and joking with the crowd around them.

'A curious phenomenon,' Zachary remarked.

Elinor stared into the glowing embers. She had been so close to the dancers that she could have reached out a hand and touched them, and the heat from the fire was burning her skin and making it uncomfortable to be so near it.

'It isn't possible!' she exclaimed.

Zachary laughed. 'They don't feel a thing!' he assured her.

'Maybe not!' she retorted crisply. 'They were all in a trance, but how did their clothes manage to escape?'

Zachary shrugged. 'I haven't the faintest idea!' he admitted. 'Mind over matter, I suppose.'

They laughed together and began to push their way back out of the crowd. They thought they had seen all they wanted to. It had been an awe-inspiring spectacle, but it was not one that they wanted to continue watching, it was so uncanny and, in a way, inhuman.

On the edge of the crowd stood an ancient Negress, trying to peer over the heads of the people in front of her. Automatically, Elinor stood back to encourage her to take her place and the Negress said something to her, with a broad, flashing smile.

'What did she say?' Elinor asked Zachary.

He laughed. 'She says that she was once an *arifa* herself, but that she is too old for that sort of thing now. Don't you believe it,' he added, 'one sniff of coloured incense and she would be well away!'

'I wish I could understand it better,' Elinor answered, still puzzled as to why they should do it.

'I should think they get a terrific physical release from it,' he said seriously. 'There's much the same sort of thing going on in Haiti and all round there. Why not here?'

'Why not?' she echoed him.

After the hot glow of the fire, the streets seemed darker than ever. Elinor held tightly on to Zachary's hand in case she got parted from him, or tripped over the uneven patches in the narrow streets.

'I'm glad I've seen it,' she said at last.

He looked amused. 'Why?' he asked.

'I don't know,' she replied honestly. 'Sometimes we think all mankind is exactly the same. It's rather nice to know that there are some differences left!'

He laughed. 'Very nice!' he agreed. 'I often think so myself!'

They paused at the corner of the street while Zachary got his bearings as to which way they should go. He hesitated only for a moment, but it was long enough for someone to come out of the shadows and to brush against them. Elinor felt only the brush of his cloak, but Zachary almost doubled up and had to lean against one of the buildings for support.

'What happened?' Elinor asked in sharp alarm.

Zachary shook his head.

'A Blue Man,' he whispered.

'So?' Elinor whispered back.

Zachary grimaced with pain. He must be winded, Elinor thought. She stood closer to him and took some of his weight on her own shoulders.

'Hang on to me!' she commanded him. 'I'll support you and we can get home.'

His eyes laughed at her before he doubled up with pain again. He recovered himself with dignity and held something in his hand out for her to look at.

'Ever seen anything like that?' he asked her.

She held out her hand and he dropped the object he was holding into her open palm. She examined it closely and was surprised to see that it was a piece of jewellery, done in enamel, with a number of intricate designs carefully interwoven.

'What is it?' she asked.

Zachary took it from her again and put it into his pocket. 'It's the sort of jewellery the Chleuh excel at,' he said slowly. 'You can buy it easily in the south. Their women wear a lot of it.'

'But that wasn't a Chleuh!' Elinor protested.

'No,' Zachary agreed. 'That was a Blue Man, a Tuareg. But their lands march side by side down there.'

Elinor wrinkled up her brow. 'They were Chleuh who came for you that night,' she remembered hesitantly.

'So they were!' Zachary agreed, as though he had not been thinking about *that* at all! 'Never mind, perhaps it was a genuine accident and he didn't see me coming.'

But Elinor couldn't believe that and she didn't think that he did either.

'I wish you'd tell me all about those two years,' she begged him. But he shook his head.

'One day!' he promised lightly. 'Look, we're nearly home!'

It was something of a relief to be back in the safety of Zachary's garden. Someone had cleared away the dishes they had used for their evening meal and had brought a couple of hurricane lamps to light the small square.

Zachary pulled the piece of jewellery out of his pocket again and examined it more closely in the flickering light.

'Would you like it as a keepsake?' he asked her.

She bent down beside him and gazed at the enamelled surface again. It was beautiful in its own way. Primitive, with edges that could have been smoother and better fashioned to lie against the skin, it had a luminous quality and an originality that spoke of a true artist.

'Don't you want it?' she asked him almost humbly.

He frowned down at it, as if he was unable to make up his mind. Then, almost as if it had stung him, he pushed it into her hands.

'No, you keep it!' he said bitterly. 'But keep it safe. It probably cost some poor devil a lot!'

Elinor looked at him, thoroughly puzzled.

'You're not still in danger, are you, Zachary?' she asked him quietly.

He threw back his head with the nervous gesture of someone who is not very sure of anything but who will be independent till the last.

'Of course not! I'm quite all right now.' He stood up straight and his eyes were lost in shadows. 'Don't look so concerned, darling,' he said gently. 'I know how to look after myself.'

'But do you?'

He smiled and she wished more than ever she knew what he was thinking. He was so mysterious and she knew that in some way she had failed him, though as he refused to tell her anything she didn't see what else she could have done.

'Of course I can!' he laughed at her. 'I know how to look after my own very well indeed!'

Elinor shrugged, remembering how thin he was and how vulnerable he had looked when that stranger had winded him in the street.

'I hope so,' she said doubtfully, and then on a sudden note of anxiety: 'Zachary, you will take care?'

He nodded, without speaking. He put his hands on her shoulders and turned her face to him. For a wild, mad moment, she thought he was going to kiss her, but he didn't.

'I think I'd better take you back to your father,' he said.

She was disappointed, there was no doubt about that. And that made her cross with herself. She had to make up her mind one way or the other. She couldn't shilly-shally about, half willing to accept Zachary back on any terms. No, she decided with a fierceness that surprised her, she had made her decision. Her marriage to Zachary had been a disaster, so why should she feel such a traitor when he looked at her like that? *He* obviously felt as free as air, free enough to flirt with his cousin at any rate.

'Yes, you'd better take me home,' she agreed wearily.

Only somehow, over the evening, her father's house didn't seem like home to her any more. She much preferred the fairyland quality of Zachary's house, which had been bought for her. She clutched the enamel necklace very tightly, so that she could feel its jagged edges cutting into her fingers. At least she had that to take with her, she thought.

'Zachary——' she began.

He looked inquiringly at her.

'Nothing!' she said. She could hardly tell him that she didn't want to go back to her father. That she wanted to stay there with him.

'Nothing?' he mocked her, pulling his *djellabah* closer round his body. Elinor blushed at the tone in his voice and was angrier with herself than ever.

'Nothing at all!' she said.

CHAPTER EIGHT

MR. KENDON strolled slowly through the garden with his daughter at his side.

'I've arranged for the solicitor fellow to come this afternoon,' he told her.

Elinor sighed. 'I wish you hadn't, Father,' she said.

'Why not?' he shot at her.

'I don't know,' Elinor admitted. 'I'd rather have had time to get used to the idea that Zachary is still alive before I see solicitors and that sort of thing.'

Her father grunted. 'Can't put these things off, you know, dear. Your passport says you're a widow, don't forget! That has to be changed, at least.'

'I suppose so,' she admitted unhappily. 'But nothing more than that, Father. Not yet!'

Mr. Kendon shrugged. 'Just as you like. Though I can't see any point in putting things off myself. I'd like to have everything settled before—soon!'

Elinor felt more badly than ever.

'Father, is there something wrong?' she asked him. 'You're not well, are you? Zachary says it's high blood pressure. Is it more than that?'

Her father's face reddened with anger.

'There's nothing the matter with me! Nothing at all! And I'll thank you not to discuss it with that jackanapes, if you don't mind!'

'But he's a very good doctor!' Elinor protested. 'You have to admit that!'

'I don't wish to discuss it!' Mr. Kendon cut her off. 'I have no interest in Zachary Wild. I should like to have the whole affair finished and done with so that I could forget all about him, and I strongly advise you to do the same!'

'But I can't,' she said gently.

'Then you can't,' her father admitted. 'But don't discuss me with him, or my business either!'

She looked at him, bewildered.

'Of course not, if you don't want me to. But it won't be easy.' She took a deep breath. 'I'm going to work for him until I can get things settled in my own mind!'

'I'll arrange a proper job for you,' he retorted fiercely. 'I know them well at the hospital. You'll get a decent rate of pay there—something you can begin to live on.'

Elinor shook her head. 'Zachary is going to pay me full rates,' she said stubbornly. 'I'm going to work for him no matter what. I owe him that much at least!'

'You don't owe him anything!' her father returned in a stifled voice. 'Nothing at all! It wasn't you who deserted him!'

'No,' she agreed. 'But I don't yet know why he disappeared. Do you?'

Mr. Kendon shook his head.

'I don't want to know,' he said abruptly. He looked sad and even disillusioned. 'You know,' he went on, 'for the first time I regret coming to Morocco. The Moors don't think as we do, and I regret to say that young man is a Moor in everything but the blood that runs in his veins.'

Elinor was intrigued. 'Oh, do you think so?' she said.

Mr. Kendon grunted. 'I do think so. But I certainly don't mean it in the silly romantic way that you imagine!'

Elinor laughed. 'Somehow a nurse's training doesn't lead to a romantic view of life,' she said without bitterness, merely as if she were stating a fact.

'Nonsense!' her father retorted. 'You've always been mushy where Zachary is concerned——'

'Oh, not mushy!' she denied.

'What else? If only Gerard had been here then things might have been different. There's none of that sort of nonsense about him. He understands which things are important and which are not!'

'And Zachary doesn't?' Elinor really wanted to know. She wasn't at all sure herself about the proper priorities of things.

'If he did he would have set up his practice in Sydney, or even in the States. No one asked him to come here, did they? He'll never make his fortune out of a few tribesmen, or even the Moroccans who live in Meknes and Fez.'

'Perhaps he doesn't want to make his fortune?'

Mr. Kendon snorted. 'That's unreasonable in itself!' he exclaimed. 'Anyway, Elinor, the solicitor will be here at about four this afternoon. You're to be here, is that understood?'

Elinor nodded.

'I can manage that, I think,' she said smoothly. 'I don't suppose Zachary will hold his surgery until later in the evening.'

'I don't care when he holds it,' her father responded. 'You're to be here!'

But to Elinor it made all the difference. She felt like a tightrope walker. If she overbalanced either way, she would hurt someone, or make them displeased with her, and just at the moment she didn't feel strong enough to withstand that displeasure. She felt as if she had entered a very long tunnel and that the glimpse of light she had seen had been no more than a mirage, she would only know what she really wanted when she came out the other side. It was no good trying to hurry herself, or to make herself fall in love with Gerard, or dwell on what she really thought about people who didn't keep their marriage vows. She didn't know what she really thought about anything at the moment!

'All right,' she said. 'I'll be there.'

Lillemor, who apparently never rose before midday, came drifting into Elinor's bedroom just before lunch. She

105

walked over to the window that overlooked the courtyard below and looked appreciatively out at the flowers and the singing birds down below.

'What a lovely room you have!' she said with frank envy.

Elinor came over and stood beside her.

'It is nice,' she agreed. 'My father bought this house when he first came to Morocco. It was madly expensive, even then, and cost him every penny he had. I used to think it was the loveliest house in the whole world, but just sometimes it all seems a bit too much. There's nothing that isn't carved or decorated in some way, is there?'

Lillemor gave a little shiver of content.

'I think it's gorgeous! It's so rich! It has such atmosphere! And just listen to those darling birds singing their little hearts out!'

Elinor smiled. She knew exactly what the Australian girl meant, but there were times when one wanted a little less icing and a little more beauty of line all the same. Or had she only thought so since she had seen Zachary's house, she mocked herself.

'Why don't you go down to the patio?' she asked her guest. 'One of the servants will bring you a drink.'

Lillemor shook her head. 'Why do you call it the patio?' she asked curiously. 'Your father calls it something else.'

Elinor laughed. 'The court of the sun,' she translated the Arabic term that her father used. 'It was once called that when this house was occupied by one of the sons of Moulay Ismael. It was called that because the sun always finds its way into it no matter what the time of day. My father is very proud of it.'

'The court of the sun,' Lillemor repeated. 'Doesn't it sound dazzling and splendid?'

Elinor nodded slowly, thinking back to the day when she had seen it at its very best, with the lingering scent of the orange blossom heavy on the air and the sound of the birds in the background. It had been the day she had married Zachary.

'I always have loved it,' she said.

Lillemor looked at her curiously. Her pale eyes seemed almost to guess what her hostess was thinking and they flickered away to the courtyard and she laughed softly under her breath.

'Well, never mind all that now,' she said. 'I came with a message. Zachary has asked me to have tea with him. He said he'd forgotten to give you a time to get ready for his surgery. Could you be there at half-past five?'

Elinor nodded. Half-past five would suit her very well, she thought grimly. She would just have had time to recover from the solicitor's visit.

'I'll be there,' she said aloud.

Lillemor's smile showed her neat, white teeth and the tip of her tongue.

'You won't mind, will you, if Zachary isn't exactly *prompt*?' she murmured. 'He *thinks* he's going to be there on the dot, but I shan't nearly have finished with him by then!'

Elinor discovered that she did mind, very much indeed, but there didn't seem to be any point in saying so.

'I expect I shall be able to find my own way about the surgery,' she answered. 'Keep him as long as you like!'

Lillemor's eyes flashed with laughter.

'I knew you'd understand, darling!' she said gracefully, and wandered out as confidently as she had come in. Elinor watched her go. She wished hopelessly that the other girl would be called back to Australia, or would go anywhere rather than remain anywhere near Zachary. It wasn't only that Elinor was jealous of her. She didn't trust her either, for Lillemor's world only had one real inhabitant, and that was Lillemor herself.

It took a little time for her full resentment to grow about

Zachary casually sending her messages through his cousin. He could have come and told her himself, or written a note, or anything rather than let the Australian girl see that he didn't care enough to make the effort to make his own arrangements. Elinor tried not to think about it, but the hurt was still there and nothing she could do would make it go away.

The solicitor when he came was a dapper little man. It was impossible to tell from his looks if he was a Frenchman or a Moor, but his training had been entirely French.

'I hope I shall be able to be of service to you,' he greeted Elinor. His shrewd blue eyes noted the paleness of her face and the tight, worried look around her mouth. 'There is no need for me to take any action you do not wish,' he added comfortably with a sidelong glance at Mr. Kendon.

Elinor tried to smile at him.

'I'm not ready to come to a decision of any kind,' she told him. 'It's too soon!'

'Much too soon!' the solicitor agreed promptly. He smiled very gently. 'We can agree about that immediately. It is what to do in the meantime that we must consider. I understand that your husband has returned, alive?'

Elinor nodded.

'I can give you his address,' she said. 'He has set up his surgery there. I'm going to work for him today.'

Mr. Kendon grunted his disapproval from the window.

'Supposing you decide it would be better to part?' he demanded. 'What then? It would compromise any decision you made!'

'I don't think so,' Elinor said tenaciously. 'We have to face facts. And—and anyway, Zachary is never vindictive!'

The solicitor hid a smile.

'Well, Mrs. Wild, that is really neither here nor there at the moment. The thing we have to put right is that all your papers say you are a widow and you are not one yet. We shall have to rectify that first of all.'

'Yes,' Elinor agreed with relief. 'Let's concentrate on that.'

It only took a few minutes to hand over her marriage certificate, the certificate presuming Zachary's death, and her own papers to have the entry of widow altered on them.

'If anything happens,' she added at the end when the solicitor was going, 'Dr. Wild will get in touch with you. In the end it has to be up to him, doesn't it?'

The lawyer refused to commit himself.

'We shall do nothing without your consent,' he assured her.

Mr. Kendon walked with him to the door and watched him walk easily off down the street. He came back into his study where Elinor was still sitting, with a stunned and miserable look on her face.

'I wonder if he realises who's paying his fees?' he began angrily. 'I told him I wanted things settled!'

Elinor bit her lip. 'I'll pay him myself,' she told her father with decision. 'I'd much rather, because I refuse to be hurried into anything!'

Mr. Kendon glowered down at her. 'The trouble is that in spite of everything you're still in love with the fellow, isn't that it?'

Elinor rose a trifle unsteadily to her feet.

'Yes, I suppose it is,' she said gently.

'Then why don't you go back to him?' her father demanded.

Elinor winced. 'Because,' she said slowly, 'he doesn't yet trust me enough to tell me where he's been. I won't go back to him until I know!'

Mr. Kendon's lip curled with contempt.

'And don't you know that he'll never take you back unless you go without knowing?' he shouted at her. 'He's that kind of man! No consideration for his wife's feelings, only for his own! You were expected to fall into his arms and forgive him anything, and he'll never forgive you for not doing exactly that!'

Elinor summoned up a painful smile. 'Probably not,' she agreed.

The heat outside was appalling, but even so it seemed an escape from the stifling atmosphere she had left behind in her father's house. Elinor watched the sun dance on the surface of the road ahead of her and took a deep breath of relief. It was all over for the moment and she could forget all about it. Not that it was quite so easy to do just that in actual fact, but with any luck she would be so busy with Zachary that she wouldn't have time to dwell on her own dark thoughts and imaginings.

Because she was early, she loitered through the local shops, looking at this and that without any intention of buying anything at all. She paused by a metal-worker, watching the way he used his tiny hammer on the copper, hammering it into the shape of a dish. Next door was another man working with leather, and filling out the lettering in gold. It looked very magnificent, but it was work which was trying on the eyes and the man worked in such a poor light that it was a miracle that he could see anything at all.

Beyond the leather-worker was a grocer. Elinor very nearly didn't stop to look in at all, but the carefully laid out spices and sweet-smelling herbs won her interest in spite of herself. There were sacks full of *tfel*, a special type of mud that the Moors used as a shampoo and as a cosmetic for softening the skin of their faces. Before it had been broken down in hot water it looked like so many chips of Kentish coal, red rather than black, but shiny and hard.

'Come in and buy!' the shopkeeper invited her.

Elinor shook her head.

'Not just now,' she said pleasantly. She smiled at the proprietor and then looked quickly at him again. She was quite sure that he too was a Chleuḥ and she couldn't help

110

wondering if he knew about Zachary and about the strange incident of the night before. She felt in her handbag and drew out the necklace which Zachary had given her.

'I was given this,' she told him. 'Can you tell me what it means?'

The shopkeeper frowned at her.

'It is an ornament, no more than that.'

'But you do belong to the Chleuh, don't you?' she pressed him.

The Moroccan nodded. 'It is true,' he agreed. 'The necklace is typical of our jewellery,' he added a shade more reluctantly, 'but it doesn't mean anything. All our women wear similar necklaces.'

Elinor spelt out the pattern on the enamel with her finger.

'And these words don't mean anything?' she suggested hopefully.

The man took the necklace from her and frowned down at the pattern that was so beautifully executed.

'It means very little,' he assured her. 'It bears the mark of a certain man on it. Not a Chleuh!' he added quickly. 'He is no one you would have ever heard of.'

'But you have?' Elinor put in.

The man nodded his head. 'I have heard stories of this man. But he is nothing to do with the Chleuh. He probably liked our enamel work and had this piece made for himself. Perhaps he traded it for a young camel, or something like that.'

'Tell me his name,' Elinor demanded.

But the grocer would not. 'I have told you all I know,' he said firmly. 'I cannot tell you any more.'

'Is the man a Tuareg?' Elinor asked, determined not to be cheated of her discovery.

The grocer shrugged. 'I cannot tell you. Why should you want to know? It is none of your business. It is pretty and you are the new owner of it. That is enough for any woman!'

The trouble was that as far as Elinor was concerned it was by no means enough. But she realised that she would get no further with the grocer. If he knew any more he would not tell her. The men who came from the south had their own secrets and their own way of life, and they could deal harshly with those who had offended against their own particular code. The Chleuh, with their ability for making money in the cities, had little in common within their desert neighbours, the 'Blue Men', but they did occasionally trade together and they knew better than to reveal each other's secrets.

Elinor put the necklace back in her handbag.

'Thank you very much,' she said to the grocer with a smile. He nodded back to her and turned quickly to a waiting customer to serve him. Elinor thought that the customer asked him who she was, but her Arabic was not good enough to be sure. She looked him full in the face as she left the shop and was relieved to see that he was a mild-looking man dressed in a black *djellabah*, with dark glasses and a heavy stick with which he prodded the sacks beside him as if he could only see a very little and had no wish to tumble over anything. He scarcely looked the danger that she had imagined he might be for a single wild moment.

It was only when she came out of the shop that she began to doubt that she had gone the right way for Zachary's house. The Medina in Meknes was not nearly as large as the one in Fez and the alleys were wider and better planned, but even so it was easy enough to get lost and to find oneself going the wrong way and further and further away from the place one wanted.

In the end she stopped and asked a small shrouded figure who answered her readily enough in Arabic. From beneath her veil, Elinor could just glimpse the red of her hennaed hair and the soft sparkle of curiosity in the one eye she presented to the world.

'Can you direct me to the doctor's house?' Elinor asked her.

The woman nodded. 'The English doctor?' she confirmed.

Elinor wondered if Zachary would approve of that particular label, but there didn't seem to be much point in explaining that he was an Australian to the woman. Very probably she had never even heard of Australia.

'Can you show me his house?' she asked again.

The woman gave a garbled explanation of how to get there. She could not count, so she could not tell how many streets away it was. The best she could do was to tell her what landmarks to look out for. Elinor thanked her gravely and watched her as she walked on down the street, her veil pulled over her face with her right hand, looking for all the world like an animated sack of flour.

With the help of her directions Elinor found Zachary's house fairly easily. Fortunately she recognised it when she glanced down the right alleyway to see if there was anything familiar that she could remember down it. The door set in the plain wall was no different from any other, but the tips of the trees peeping over the top of the wall struck a bell and the knocker shaped into a symbol of a woman's hand for good luck convinced her that she had come to the right place.

Elinor rapped on the knocker, wondering even as she did so whether she shouldn't go to the other door where the surgery was ultimately going to be. There was a long pause and then the door was slowly opened. A young girl, dressed in a ragged skirt and jumper, stood there looking at her.

'Dr. Wild?' Elinor asked.

The girl nodded and went on standing there. She had the remains of what had once been a scarlet scarf tying back her thick black hair and her cheeks were thin and had that greenish look of ill-health that dark skins are apt to get when their owners are off colour.

'I am the new nurse,' Elinor told her with a breezy confidence she was far from feeling. But still the girl went on standing there. 'May I come in?' Elinor asked at last.

The girl shook her head.

'Dr. Wild is busy,' she said. She spoke as if the very effort of talking was a worry to her. Elinor looked at her sharply.

'Did you come to see him yourself?' she asked her.

The girl went on staring at her through unblinking eyes, not making any effort to reply.

Elinor smiled encouragingly at her and pushed the door a little further open with one hand. She could see for herself that there was nobody else inside. Still smiling at the girl, she walked firmly in through the door and shut it behind her.

'Are you a patient?' she asked over her shoulder as she made her way towards the room she and Zachary had thought would be the best one for the surgery.

The girl nodded faintly. 'My people sent me,' she explained shyly.

She was a Berber, Elinor thought as she studied her face. That accounted for the fact that she went unveiled and was prepared to have a male doctor to examine her. The poor girl looked tubercular to Elinor, but she had had very little experience of the disease in fact. There were so few cases left in England, but it abounded in the narrow dark streets of the ancient Moorish cities.

'Come with me,' Elinor bade her. The girl looked tired, but she would probably enjoy helping to set out some of the essentials ready for Zachary's surgery at half-past five. 'Do you want to help?' she asked her in a kindly tone. The girl nodded again and came along more quickly, her curious eyes darting here and there as various strange things caught her interest.

Zachary had already been busy, Elinor noted as she

entered the room. He had placed a couple of screens round some of the chairs for the women to wait behind and he had brought in several of the more heavy pieces of equipment that he would need. The largest was an X-ray screen behind which he could stand the various patients and see on the spot whether they were suffering from tuberculosis or any of the other things detectable by that means. Elinor looked at it with interest and then fell to unpacking the various boxes of instruments that were lying on the floor.

The sterilising equipment stood in one corner, and Elinor plugged it in and dropped the instruments into the water ready to boil them up. She was getting hot and she began to wish that she had brought two aprons with her, so that she could look clean and tidy when surgery actually began. She glanced at her watch once or twice and saw that the time was very nearly half-past five already. With an increasing sense of urgency she explained to the young girl the few things which remained to be done, and tried to wash the black dust off her hands and to remove the smudges from her face.

The water was cold and there was no soap that she could find. She made a mental note to bring some the following day and watched the now brown water swill away down the drain. They were lucky, she thought, that at least the plumbing worked. There were many places in Morocco still so primitive that there were no main drains or running water.

She was just drying her hands when Zachary came in.

'I was going to come and fetch you,' he said with a smile. 'I thought it would be a day or so before you would manage to find your way here on your own!'

Elinor gave him a superior smile.

'I found it easily enough,' she said. She glanced over his shoulder. 'Where's Lillemor?' she asked.

His own smile took on a tinge of mockery. 'She's waiting for me in the house. She wasn't ready to go back to you, so

I suggested she stayed on for a meal this evening.'

'I see,' Elinor said coldly.

'Do you? I wonder,' he drawled. 'My cousin is a most attractive woman and——'

'Most!' Elinor fell over herself to agree.

'And,' Zachary went on in imperturbable tones, 'attractive women like to get their own way all the time!'

'Who doesn't?' Elinor asked dryly.

Zachary grinned. 'She's useful in other ways too,' he added. 'She keeps me informed about this and that! For instance,' he said darkly, 'what you've been doing this afternoon.'

'Oh?' Elinor said lightly.

'Yes, *oh!*' he retorted. 'So you saw a solicitor?'

'Yes. Yes, I did,' Elinor admitted. 'My father asked him to come.'

'*And?*' Zachary pressed her.

'And he's going to have my passport put right,' she went on quietly. 'I couldn't go on masquerading as a widow for ever, could I?' She paused and smiled sweetly at him, admiring her own calm and collected exterior. '*And* I'm paying him myself!'

Zachary's eyes clashed with hers, but she refused to look away.

'Good,' he said. 'Then we'd better begin this surgery and get it over with.'

'Yes, sir,' she said respectfully.

CHAPTER NINE

THE surgery stretched on endlessly. There was no doubt that the young girl who had assisted Elinor with unpacking the instruments was tubercular, but there was very little that could be done about it. Elinor was surprised to learn that she was already married and the mother of two children. If she were to be given adequate rest and treatment what was to happen to the children? Zachary was depressed by his diagnosis and as kind as Elinor had ever seen a doctor be with a patient, yet the brutal fact remained that he could do very little for her.

'Come back with your husband one day soon,' he told her.

The girl nodded. 'When my husband is willing I will come,' she agreed. They both knew that it was unlikely that she would ever come again.

When she had gone Zachary sighed and studied the notes he had taken.

'We ought to do something about people like her!' he exclaimed with frustrated longing. 'The Fassi students at the Moslem university there are riddled with it too.'

'Fez has always had that reputation,' Elinor agreed. Then she tried tactfully to turn the conversation, knowing that there was nothing either of them could do at that particular moment. 'There are a lot of people waiting,' she said.

Zachary grinned at her. 'Well, that should keep us from brooding!' he agreed. 'Show the next one in.'

Those who came and waited did so because they had heard long ago about the strange English doctor who had gone among them once before, curing the more fortunate and comforting those who had left it too late, or for whom

117

there was no hope. The men sat huddled against each other on one side of the waiting room, dressed in all manner of different garbs, from the traditional Arab to the very latest copies from the swinging West. The women were mostly veiled and sat patiently and in silence behind the screens that Zachary had set up for their convenience.

One by one they went through the door to where Zachary was waiting. With the men it was reasonably simple to make a diagnosis. With the women it was often impossible as they refused to unveil, or to do anything more than to repeat a rather garbled version of their symptoms, suitably modified to be suitable for a man's ears to hear. Zachary was patient and unbelievingly sympathetic. If there was no other answer, he would encourage them to explain their illnesses to Elinor and go on from there.

On the whole it worked very well. Elinor had never known another surgery like it. She thought she had not worked so hard since she had first begun her training, and her feet and her whole body had ached with fatigue after her first day on the wards. She felt the same way now, but she was still sorry when the last man in the queue had been seen and there was nothing more to do but to clear up and lay out the trays of instruments for the following day.

Zachary washed his hands for the last time and took off his white coat, already crinkled and wet with perspiration.

'We must do something about keeping it a bit cooler in here,' he said with distaste. 'I feel as hot as you look!'

Elinor smiled. 'I should have brought a change of apron,' she said. 'I should have known I would dirty this one getting things straight!'

'And what are you going to do now?' Zachary asked her.

Elinor remembered with a renewal of hurt that he was going to spend his evening with Lillemor. She shrugged her shoulders in a deliberately casual manner.

'I think I'll go to the baths and get clean,' she said.

He grinned. 'To the *hammam*? What makes you think

it's open to women at this time?'

Elinor found herself smiling back.

'The men have it later on. I'm quite safe if I go now,' she answered him. She was enjoying the look of admiration in his eyes. Such an adventure would appeal to him, she thought, and unconsciously preened herself on having gained his favour.

'I envy you,' he said at last.

The telephone rang shrilly in the waiting room and he got up and answered it. When he came back he was frowning.

'I have to go out,' he said, glancing at his watch. 'Do you think you could take Lillemor with you? Send her back here when you've finished. I should be back myself by then.'

Elinor didn't really suppose Lillemor would want to come with her. The *hammam* was attached to the local mosque, so that the faithful could thoroughly cleanse themselves before they prayed. If the mosque was well-to-do so were the baths, but the ones that she went to were simple and plain and she was afraid that Lillemor would find them lacking in comfort and obvious hygiene.

'If she'd like to come, I don't mind,' she said aloud. She rather hoped that Lillemor would have something else to do, but Zachary had a determined jut to his chin as he went to find her and she was not altogether surprised when he came back with Lillemor already clothed for the outside streets.

'I suppose it will ruin my hair-do!' the Australian girl muttered.

'Nonsense!' said Zachary.

'I'm afraid it will,' Elinor said with greater accuracy. 'But it's worth it. I think you'll enjoy the experience!'

'It looks as though I shall have to!' Lillemor retorted balefully. 'We'll have to buy some clean flannels and towels on the way—that at least I insist on!'

Elinor obligingly agreed to that. She was wondering where Zachary was going and why he looked so nervous about it. She was getting very suspicious of his every move, she told herself crossly, and reminded herself how little men liked having to explain themselves.

'We'd better be going,' she said on a sigh.

The two girls walked side by side along the narrow streets to the mosque. They could see the outer courtyard from the street, simple and beautiful, but neither of them would have been allowed any further inside. The baths, however, were different, easily recognisable by the elaborate highly painted horseshoe door. Elinor knocked on it and walked straight through into the gloomy interior, waving to Lillemor to follow her.

'It takes getting used to,' she explained in a fierce undertone. She was a little afraid that Lillemor was going to dislike such a public form of cleansing and she didn't know what she was going to do if the other girl jibbed when once they had got started.

'I'll pay for the two of us,' she said hastily. Lillemor glanced round and shivered with pleasurable horror.

'Heavens above!' she exclaimed.

Elinor too noticed for the first time the peeling paint and the shabby look of the floor.

'There are far grander ones than these,' she told Lillemor. 'Some of them are covered in marble and are very exotic, but I always come here because I know the women here.'

Lillemor smiled faintly.

'Lead on!' she exclaimed. 'I can see I shall hate every minute of it, but I wouldn't miss it for anything!'

Elinor paid the few coins necessary to enter and received in return two piles of towels, dressing-gowns and wooden slippers to wear in the actual hot, steam-filled rooms. Gathering a bundle under either arm, she led the way into the dressing room and began to undress, clutching the dressing-gown around her. In the end she emerged in her petticoat. Lillemor, following her example, folded her clothes and put them away on a chair.

'What happens now?' she asked.

'It's just like a Turkish bath,' Elinor explained simply. 'We start off in the hottest room and then one of the masseuses comes along and washes and massages us and then we cool off and get dressed again.'

'Okay,' said Lillemor. She balanced herself uneasily on her wooden slippers and clattered across the marble floor to where Elinor was pointing to the hottest of the steam-filled rooms.

They sat for a while in silence on a concrete platform, watching the other women who had come in their family groups and had settled down to a good gossip wherever they stood. Most of them still had their petticoats on, others who had already washed stood naked with their sopping petticoats held negligently in front of them, their bronzed bodies beautifully moulded against the white walls. Against them, Elinor as always felt too white and rather unattractive. It was unfair, she thought, that even the blue-eyed Moroccans managed to have that tanned look from head to foot.

'My hair-do is well and truly ruined already!' Lillemor complained after a few moments.

Elinor felt her own wet hair and shook it free, shaking the sweat out of her eyes at the same time.

'I missed this in England,' she said as she stretched her limbs. 'I feel so clean after I've been here!'

'I suppose Zachary comes here too?' Lillemor asked innocently. The hot steam made it difficult to breathe and she was madly uncomfortable sitting on the concrete platform and wondering what was going to happen to her.

'I suppose so,' Elinor agreed, amused. 'I really couldn't tell you.'

She found that she was hot enough and more than ready for the dwarf-like woman who came to fetch her for her massage and hair-washing. Each of the women who worked there had her own regular clients whom she jealously guarded. The tips and the interest in her own customers made the job a sought-after one among the widows of the district. It was considered decidedly unethical to steal someone else's customer and in actual fact it happened very seldom. Elinor's masseuse greeted her with delight, her two remaining teeth showing like two yellow fangs between her wrinkled lips.

'It has been a long time since you last came to us!' she exclaimed with real pleasure.

'I have been in England,' Elinor told her.

The woman nodded sagely.

'I had heard,' she answered. 'And I heard about your husband, now returned to you, thanks be to Allah!'

'Allah is great!' Elinor responded with Arabic courtesy.

Lillemor, now almost hotter than she could bear, came over to hear what they were talking about.

'Doesn't she speak any French?' she complained after a while.

Elinor shook her head. 'No, she has to put up with my limited Arabic!' she laughed.

Lillemor looked disappointed. 'Zachary says you speak it quite well,' she said slowly.

'Enough,' Elinor agreed. 'I can manage as long as the person is talking directly to me—about something I know about, of course. I can't discuss camels or anything like that!'

The masseuse motioned to Elinor to sit down and pulled her petticoat off her back with the ease of one who is accustomed to dealing with wet nylon all day long. She picked up a bucket of hot water and sluiced it over Elinor's naked body, before she began to soap her and to rub the dirt out of her skin with a coarse black flannel.

'They tell me your husband returned in very bad condition,' she muttered in Elinor's ear. 'I have heard all about

122

his back! He came here as soon as he got back to Meknes.'

Elinor stiffened. His back? she wondered. The woman pushed her into a more relaxed position and went on talking.

'They treated his back as he asked, but it was still painful when he left,' she said.

'Who did it?' Elinor asked in the same urgent whisper.

'Who knows?' the old woman retorted. 'He knows better than to talk where his words will be repeated.'

And that place certainly wouldn't be the baths, Elinor thought. As with all people who cannot read, or can only read a little, their gossip was their morning newspaper as well as everything else. News could travel faster through the *souks* of Morocco than a man could walk.

'What's she talking about?' Lillemor asked discontentedly. 'I'm getting bored as well as hot!'

'Perhaps you should have had her services first,' Elinor said sympathetically, and laughed when Lillemor shook her head.

'Certainly not! I want to see what happens to you first!'

Elinor rolled over on the concrete. It smelt of steam and hot water and a little of soap and henna. She made herself comfortable while the woman kneaded her flesh into softness and complete relaxation.

'Who looks after my husband?' she asked the woman sleepily.

'My brother-in-law. But he can tell you nothing. His head is as thick as the concrete floor!'

Elinor sighed. Perhaps he wouldn't talk, but she would certainly get some explanation out of Zachary. She would go back to his house with Lillemor, she decided, and she would ask him then, while she still had the courage to insist on having some kind of an answer from him. If his back needed treatment then she would give it to him. She was a trained nurse, after all, and could manage it a great deal better than most.

'What's she saying now?' Lillemor asked impatiently.

Elinor grinned lazily. 'That she's glad my husband has come home to me,' she said.

Lillemor frowned. 'I suppose she thinks she's being polite,' she said. 'If she knows so much about you, she must know that he hasn't really come back to you at all! Perhaps that's why she looks at me in such a peculiar way!'

'She doesn't!' Elinor defended the Moroccan woman. 'She only wants to know all about you—where you come from, how many children you have, why you're not married.'

'Then you can tell her I'm not married because you took the only man I ever wanted to marry!' Lillemor burst out crossly.

Elinor flushed. 'I can hardly tell her that,' she said. 'She wouldn't understand.'

Lillemor pulled her own petticoat off and doused her body down with hot water. She felt better and considerably less prickly and she sat down again, a peculiar smile on her face.

'You don't really understand yourself, do you?' she said.

Elinor shrugged. She felt pleasantly sleepy and completely relaxed. The Moroccan woman was the best masseuse she had ever known, finding each muscle and each tight corner. She was sorry when at last she had finished and cried to her to sit up again so that she could wash her hair. The woman padded off with a tin mug in one hand to half fill it with *tfel*, the soft stone they used for washing hair, breaking it down in the hot water until she could pour it on to Elinor's head and rub until the hair was soft and shiny in a way that no other shampoo seemed to succeed in making it.

Lillemor looked on with interest.

'That I am looking forward to!' she exclaimed.

'Yes,' Elinor said. 'The whole thing gives one a lovely feeling of well-being.' She submitted to having her hair washed and rinsed several times and finally wound into a towel to dry. 'Your turn!' she said to Lillemor.

The Australian girl found it better than she had expected. In Sydney she had often had a Turkish bath followed by a massage and she had looked on it as the height of luxury. It seemed odd that here they did the same thing as a matter of course. Not for the first time, she envied Elinor living in Morocco and being so much at home there. It made Zachary seem more important than ever to her.

Elinor rubbed her hair and waited for the other girl to be finished. The masseuse asked her a string of questions about her new client with a quick-eyed interest that missed nothing. Elinor couldn't help wondering what she had already heard about her and how much she was tactfully keeping to herself.

'My husband brought me a Chleuh necklace,' Elinor told her, almost by the way, as if she had suddenly thought of it.

The woman became wary, though she still nodded and smiled.

'It's very pretty,' Elinor went on casually. 'I'll show you when we go back to the dressing-room.'

'I am sure he is very generous,' the woman answered. 'Was he with the Chleuh?'

Elinor shook her head. 'No, I don't think so.'

The two yellow teeth came very near to Elinor's ear. She was aware of the woman's sympathy, almost as if she had touched her and she was grateful.

'He will tell you all in his own good time,' she said softly, and the harsh Arabic syllables sounded as beautiful as the poetry the story-tellers recited in the squares for money.

'When he is ready,' Elinor agreed. She smiled impudently at the woman. 'But it is hard for a woman to be patient,' she said.

The woman cackled with laughter. 'You could inquire

from one who knows these things,' she suggested. 'There is a man in the street next to mine who can see anything one wishes to know, but he is expensive. He would be more costly for a stranger.'

For a moment Elinor was tempted. She had heard of the strange powers that some Moors claimed to have, but she didn't feel that she could ask this man to look into Zachary's past for her. If he did know, it might be something Zachary had no wish for her to know, and if he didn't know, he would make something up and she would be misled for nothing.

'No,' she said aloud. 'I must wait—and wait!'

'The time will go soon. When your husband is no longer disturbed by evil fears, you will go to him and the children will come. You will see how it will be!'

Elinor frowned and found that she was frowning at Lillemor. It might come right, she thought. It could have done, but now that Lillemor was here and wanting Zachary, she was almost sure that she had already lost. But she wouldn't give in easily—nothing and nobody could make her do that!

As soon as Lillemor was ready, the masseuse fetched them more dry towels, hurrying them into their wooden sandals and leading the way back to the dressing-room.

'Be careful on the soapy floor,' she warned them. 'It is easy to slip!'

The two girls held hands until they reached the cool dressing-room. It was a glorious feeling, a little like the first swim in summer, when one's body is suddenly more mobile and freer than one can remember feeling before.

Elinor threw herself on to one of the divans and smiled up at Lillemor.

'Do you want something to drink?' she asked her.

They both settled for a Fanta orange drink which the masseuse brought them and opened for them, thrusting two straws into the neck of either bottle. Elinor paid her for

126

them and, at the same time, tipped her for her services.

'It has been good to be back, to come here again,' she said as she handed over the money.

The two yellow teeth became more evident than ever.

'It is good you should be here, near your husband,' she responded. 'Go with God!' She disappeared into the swirling steam of the baths in search of more customers, her skirt rucked up across her loins and her naked breasts swinging free to be better able to cope with the water and the heat.

Lillemor sat carefully on the edge of the divan and sipped her orange drink. Elinor wondered what she was thinking about and hoped against hope that it was not of Zachary.

'How long are you staying, now that you know that Zachary is all right?' she asked abruptly.

Lillemor lifted her well-plucked eyebrows a fraction.

'Has that got anything to do with you?' she asked.

'A little,' Elinor answered her carefully. 'You are staying with us.'

Lillemor laughed. 'I'll go and stay with Zachary if you'd rather!' she retorted with supreme confidence.

'Don't be silly!' Elinor said patiently. 'That wasn't what I meant at all!'

Lillemor smiled a superior little smile. 'I'm fully aware of that! What you mean is only too obvious, only this time I'm not thousands of miles away in Australia. I'm right here on your doorstep. If you want Zachary, you try and get him! It will be over my dead body!'

Elinor wondered if that was precisely what she had meant.

'I have certain advantages——' she began uncertainly.

'From where I'm sitting,' Lillemor retorted, 'you haven't one! Why don't you go and play your father's game with Gerard Roche?'

Elinor didn't answer. She pulled herself off the divan and

127

started to dress. The only reply she could think of was one that she would never have dreamed of giving voice to, but the truth was that, after Zachary, Gerard Roche seemed quite incredibly dull.

When they had both dressed, they went out into the street and Elinor started back to Zachary's house.

'If you point me in the right direction, I expect I could find the way by myself,' Lillemor drawled languidly.

'It's terribly easy to get lost!' Elinor warned. 'I think it's better if I see you to the door.'

In actual fact she wasn't prepared to brook any argument about the matter. She was going to see Zachary and she was going to see him then no matter what! She had to see him and that was that.

It was completely dark outside and the landmarks she had noted carefully before were now impossible to see. As always, Elinor liked to see the women lighting their fires in their small braziers, sometimes getting one of their children to fan the flames into hot coals ready for cooking the evening meal. Here and there a café's glare of lights broke into the darkness, where the men gathered to drink their mint tea and gossip with one another about the events of the day. It would have been easy to have been afraid in such surroundings, but Elinor knew better than to think that any man would stop her on those narrow streets. She was safer there than she would have been in many places in England. But she couldn't help rather enjoying Lillemor's fears all the same. It was not often that the other girl's confidence was shaken when her own was intact and she had every intention of making the most of the situation.

'Have we far to go?' Lillemor asked as Elinor paused at a corner in the street.

'I think it's down here,' Elinor said doubtfully. She glanced down the narrow street and then walked boldly down it. Zachary's door stood out for her now and she could recognise it with relative ease. 'Here we are!' she called back to Lillemor.

The Australian girl came running. Elinor knocked on the door and within seconds Zachary had flung it open and they stood in the warm comfort of his house.

'Had a good time?' he asked Lillemor. His eyes were dark with amusement as he ran a careless hand through her still damp hair. 'You look clean enough to eat!' he added cheerfully.

Elinor stood and watched the scene. Lillemor's toss of the head was also an invitation, she thought bitterly, and wished that she hadn't noticed Zachary's quickening interest as he looked at the other girl.

'Zachary!' she said rather more strongly than she had intended. His amused eyes rested on her for an instant and then flickered back to Lillemor. 'Zachary, I've got to talk with you for a moment!'

His eyes met hers again, but this time there was no amusement in them.

'What about?' he asked cautiously.

But she wouldn't answer him. Instead she walked into the surgery and waited, with a confidence she had acquired in the hospital in London rather than one she was actually feeling, for him to come after her. He came slowly, apologising to Lillemor as he left her alone. He looked angry and the thin, angular lines to his face were so stern that Elinor almost changed her mind about speaking to him at all.

'Well? What is it?' he asked testily.

Elinor clasped her hands together behind her back.

'It's about your back,' she said bravely.

'My back?' he repeated.

Elinor glared at him and then, quite suddenly, she lost her temper.

'Don't pretend with me!' she snapped at him. 'I suppose you think I can be hoodwinked as easily as if—as if——'

'As if what?' he shouted back.

'As if I weren't your wife!'

There was a long silence while he stood there looking at her. She couldn't read his thoughts and she could feel her own confidence oozing away beneath his regard.

'It's ridiculous!' she went on. 'Getting anyone to put ointment on it, just as if nothing was the matter at all!'

'Nothing much is!' he retorted. 'And how do you know about it anyway?'

'I was told,' Elinor informed him grimly. 'And as for it being nothing, you can take off your shirt and I'll have a look for myself!'

For a moment she thought he was going to refuse, but then quite suddenly he gave way. The lines of fatigue that had been gone for a moment seemed to be etched into his face and she longed to take it between her hands and to kiss him until he felt better. But she couldn't do that, so she turned her back instead while he took off his shirt. When she turned round he was adjusting the light so that she could see better. Across his back were lines of deep red welts, raw and painful, but no longer very recent.

'How long ago did this happen?' she asked, and her voice betrayed some of the horror she was feeling.

He shrugged his shoulders.

'About a week ago.' He busied himself in the medicine cupboard, looking for a suitable ointment for her to anoint him with. 'Actually,' he added, 'it was worth it, but you wouldn't understand that.'

She took the ointment from him with hands that trembled.

'No, I wouldn't,' she said.

CHAPTER TEN

ELINOR had almost finished anointing Zachary's back when Lillemor came bursting into the surgery.

'What are you two whispering about?' she demanded, and came to a full stop as she caught sight of the welts on Zachary's back.

'I suppose she knows what she's doing?' she went on with a bleak nod in Elinor's direction.

Zachary grinned quite cheerfully. 'She knows all right!' he assured her. 'She has the hands of a true Florence Nightingale.'

Elinor smiled too. There was no need to let the Australian girl know how she would be haunted by the sight of Zachary's back for as long as she lived.

'Why don't you wait outside?' she suggested.

Lillemor turned her back on her.

'That's what you'd like!' she exclaimed petulantly. 'I have no doubt! But if you can take it, so can I!'

Zachary grinned happily at them both. 'Girls! Girls!' he drawled. 'No quarrelling, please!'

Elinor resisted the temptation to give him a sharp pat on the shoulder.

'You be quiet!' she said instead. 'You're the patient!'

She finished his back and bandaged it neatly so that the ointment wouldn't get on his shirt and so that nothing else would rub it. He put his shirt on again and thanked her warmly, but she was busy washing her hands, which was a nice excuse for not looking at him again.

'You'd better get on with your meal,' she told him abruptly. 'Lillemor is probably hungry after her bath.'

'Yes, I am. I'm starving!' Lillemor exclaimed, glad of

131

the excuse to have him to herself. 'Come on, Zac!'

Elinor refused to look up. She heard them go out of the surgery and close the door after them. Only then did she glance at herself in the looking glass over the basin. She was surprised to see that she was crying.

Elinor ran the whole way home. She arrived breathless and with her hair flying at her father's house and went straight out to the patio to catch her breath before she went upstairs to change. Her father was out and the house seemed strangely quiet without him. She sat down in one of the chairs and looked up at the starlit sky above her. She was tired, terribly tired, and it seemed almost an effort to stay awake. In fact she might have slept if Gerard had not come in at that moment and come out to the patio too.

'Hullo,' he greeted her stiffly. 'How's the working world?'

Elinor smiled feebly up at him. 'Exhausting!' she said.

He stood stiffly over her, broodily staring down at her.

'You don't have to do it,' he said.

'Possibly not,' she agreed dryly. 'But I need the money. I can't go on for ever without any!'

'Your father would help you for a while,' he suggested.

'He might. I'd rather fend for myself.'

'By working for *him*?'

Elinor smiled briefly. 'Why not?'

'You know why not! It's intolerable!'

Elinor blinked up at him. 'I'm sorry, Gerard,' she said. 'Truly I am, but there's no need for you to feel so badly about it, is there? You mustn't let my father steamroller you into anything you'll regret. We need time, both of us, and we have all the time in the world, haven't we?'

'I suppose so,' he said blankly. 'I can't help thinking you're weakening as far as Zachary is concerned!'

Elinor stared at him thoughtfully.

'I don't know,' she said at last. 'I don't know what I feel

exactly. But I don't really believe in divorce, do you? It doesn't seem to me to answer anything.'

'It could do!' he insisted.

But Elinor shook her head. 'Not for me. I don't know about Zachary, or what he wants, but I wouldn't go through with a divorce just for myself.'

'I see,' Gerard said stiffly. 'I suppose I should thank you for telling me!'

'I'm sorry,' she said again, inadequately.

'It doesn't matter,' he said. 'As a matter of fact I'm going south to buy some camel skins from the nomads. It will make a change. It could make a change for both of us, if you'd like to come?'

Elinor hesitated. 'I don't know,' she said. 'May I think about it?'

Gerard shrugged. 'Think all you like!' he said.

The easy feel to their relationship seemed to have disappeared completely. Idly, Elinor shut her eyes and leaned back in her chair, wriggling her shoulder-blades into a more comfortable position. Perhaps she had lost her touch, she thought, and would never be completely easy with anyone again. The thought made her smile at herself. How ridiculous one could be when everything wasn't going speedily in the direction one demanded of it. She would have to wait on Zachary and he wouldn't be hurried, so she might as well get used to the idea.

'Who else will be going?' she asked Gerard. Perhaps, after all, it would be a good thing to get away for a while.

'Anyone you care to invite,' Gerard answered. 'I'm taking a couple of jeeps, so there's plenty of room.'

Elinor yawned and felt considerably better. 'I'll think about it,' she said.

Her father didn't come in to dinner. He telephoned to say he had been delayed with his friends and that he would not be back until late.

'Is Gerard there?' he asked.

'Yes, he is,' Elinor agreed.

Her father's voice sounded pleased and quite light-hearted. 'That's good,' he said. 'May as well see all of him that you can. He's going south on an errand for me.'

'Yes, I know,' Elinor told him. 'He's asked me to go along.'

'And are you going?'

But Elinor still hadn't made up her mind. 'I don't know,' she said. 'There's time yet to make up my mind.'

Her father grunted. He seemed pretty sure that she would go when it came to it. Elinor replaced the receiver carefully. She wondered if her father had thought up this whole trip to get her away from her new job. It was more than possible, but at that moment she didn't care. She still hadn't decided to go.

There was no doubt that Lillemor wanted to go, however. She came in just as Elinor and Gerard were finishing dinner. Elinor could feel her spirits lifting as she saw her. She hadn't been with Zachary very long, she thought with triumph, and chided herself for being so small-minded.

'I—I hope I'm not interrupting anything,' Lillemor said as she walked into the patio.

Gerard rose to his feet, flushing a little.

'N-nothing!' he assured her.

'Gerard is going south on a trip,' Elinor explained. 'He says we can go too if we want to.' She ignored Gerard's glowering expression. 'Do you want to go?' she asked Lillemor sweetly.

The Australian girl was immediately enthusiastic.

'I'd love it! Where are we going?'

Gerard explained briefly if rather sulkily that the nomads in the south bred camels and would sometimes sell the uncured skins at a very reasonable price. He was going south to see what he could buy, bringing the skins back north with him to have them properly cured.

'I want to get going as soon as possible,' he added, half

hoping to put the Australian girl off. 'And *very* early in the morning!'

Lillemor seemed quite unaware that this was intended as a gibe at her.

'Lovely!' she said again. 'I'll be packed and ready whenever you are. Tomorrow?'

Gerard flushed again. 'No, not tomorrow,' he said unpleasantly. 'It will have to be the day after. We'll leave first thing.'

'We'll be ready,' the two girls assured him, and immediately started to discuss the intricacies of which clothes they would take with them and what they could safely leave behind.

'I'm glad it's the day after tomorrow,' Elinor sighed. 'I still have to ask Zachary if I can go.'

'Oh, that!' Lillemor said casually. 'He can hardly refuse, can he?'

But Elinor wasn't quite so sure when she made her way to Zachary's surgery the following day. He might quite easily decide that her work came first, before any joy-rides around the country.

'You look thoughtful,' he said when she joined him in the surgery. 'Something on your mind?'

'Uh-huh. Your back first of all!'

He smiled at her with real affection. He had often looked at her like that once, she remembered, with that slight pull to the corners of his eyes as though he was laughing at them both at the same time, but in a nice way, in a way she could like.

'It's better,' he told her.

'I'll see that for myself,' she said briskly.

He made a face at her. 'Yes, nurse!' He took off his shirt and silently handed her the ointment.

It was true, his back was better. She took off the bandages with the very greatest care and was pleased to see how the skin was knitting together. In another day or so

135

there would be only the scars to see.

'Gerard,' she said loudly because she had a feeling it would sound better that way, 'is going on a trip to the south, to buy skins from the Tuareg.' She felt Zachary stiffen under her fingers. 'Lillemor and I have been invited to go too.'

'Oh?' he said smoothly. 'Do you really want to go?'

'Yes, I do,' she said.

'All right.' He turned his head and looked at her. 'We'll shut up shop for a day or two and I'll come along too.'

Elinor very nearly dropped the ointment. She made a hasty save and caught it against her apron. Some of it had spilt, making a greasy mark on the starchy whiteness, and she frowned at it and dabbed at it with her finger.

'Why do you want to come?' she asked.

Zachary grinned at her, not at all put out.

'I have some unfinished business there,' he said. 'Why are you going?'

Elinor shrugged. 'For the trip!' she said airily.

He gave her a suspicious look, but said nothing. She thought uneasily of the necklace he had given her and, somehow, her thinking about it seemed to put it into his mind as well.

'I suppose you're going to poke your nose into my affairs,' he said. 'Can't you wait for me to tell you?'

She shook her head. 'You expect me to take everything on trust!' she exclaimed. 'If you explain, I have to be properly grateful! If you don't, I must accept it and pretend that everything is just as it was! Well, I can't! I can't!'

He took the ointment out of her hands and put it back on the shelf, putting on his shirt with an easy cat-like movement.

'I'll tell you when it's safe for you to know. And for heaven's sake leave that necklace behind on this trip!'

'Why?' she demanded. 'I want to know what it means. It

has somebody's symbol on it.'

'How did you find that out?' he asked her.

'Easily enough,' she answered. 'As a matter of fact I asked a grocer what it meant. Is that where you were, Zachary? In the south?'

He looked thoughtfully down at his hands.

'More or less,' he said.

It was late when the surgery was finished. Elinor refused Zachary's offer of a drink and began to think about going home to pack.

'What are you going to eat?' she asked him as she fastened her cloak around her shoulders.

'I'll get something out,' he muttered. 'There's a pretty good restaurant just round the corner.'

She looked at him doubtfully. He would never put on any flesh if he didn't eat properly.

'See that you do!' she said.

He laughed at her, his eyes glinting.

'You're in a very wifely mood!' he teased her.

She blushed, because she thought he might kiss her, and hastily departed. But she felt warm and comforted inside as she made her way home through the narrow ill-lit streets. It was nice somehow just thinking about Zachary.

It seemed a miracle in the morning that they should all be packed and ready when Gerard brought round the two jeeps to the front door. Most of the luggage seemed to belong to the two girls, the men had no more than a change of clothing and their washing and shaving things. It was less easy too when one had to dress for the jeep and take dresses and stockings as well. Elinor had been pleased to get everything she needed into a small suitcase—Lillemor had not been so sparing and had two cases, both of them crammed to overflowing with toilet objects and various remedies against the sun.

Zachary leaned negligently against the doorpost.

'Do you want me to drive one of those for you?' he asked Gerard, pointing to the two jeeps.

Gerard barely looked up. 'No. We're all going to travel in one and the luggage and the guides can go in the other.'

Zachary said nothing. Elinor suspected that he didn't approve of the arrangement and she wasn't at all sure that she did either.

'Who are the guides?' she asked.

Gerard frowned at her. 'They're all right!' he insisted. 'I've got one of your father's men and a Tarqui friend of his to translate when we get to the Tuareg country.'

'What on earth is a Tarqui?' Lillemor chimed in, amused by the name.

'It's the singular of Tuareg,' Elinor explained. 'They're the "Blue Men".'

'Oh, I see,' Lillemor said vaguely. She was very little wiser, but she didn't really want to know. To her they were all strange and picturesque and that was all she wanted to know.

'They sound terribly romantic!' she said.

Elinor laughed. 'They are in a way. The men go veiled and the women wear their faces bare. They are really one of the white races of the Sahara, but the dye in their veils isn't fast and after a while they get a blue tinge to their skin, hence their nickname.'

Zachary listened to Elinor's explanation as though he were not listening at all.

'If we're all going in the one jeep we'd better set off,' he suggested calmly. 'If we follow one another too closely the dust will be terrible when we get off the good roads.'

Gerard almost stamped his foot.

'We're leading the way!' he snapped. 'We can worry about the dust when we get to it.'

'It'll still be there for the second car,' Zachary drawled easily.

'Not for miles yet!' Gerard retorted. 'I'm driving the

138

first vehicle and Muhammed the second. We can change over later when we get tired.'

'Just as you like,' agreed Zachary amiably. He climbed into the back seat of the first jeep and drew out a long strip of cotton cloth which he wound expertly round his head, looking just like any Arab. He was so busy doing this that Elinor thought for a moment that he hadn't seen the Tarqui guide who came and stood by the second jeep. The man waited patiently, his face almost entirely hidden by his *litham*, the blue veil that was stretched across his face. Zachary looked up suddenly and Elinor realised that he had been watching them all carefully all the time.

'Hullo, Ammamun,' he said.

The Tarqui started and pulled his veil yet higher up his face.

'Si Zachary,' he responded slowly. His uneasiness was obvious even to Gerard.

'Do you know this man?' he asked Zachary.

'We've met,' Zachary agreed.

The Tarqui spoke earnestly to Muhammed, trying to get out of the job he had taken on.

'Look here,' said Gerard to Zachary, his annoyance getting the better of him, 'I wish you wouldn't upset everybody. If I've got to choose between the two of you, I'm taking the guide. So you'd better get things sorted out.'

Zachary nodded pleasantly. He said something abruptly in Ammamun's own language and the Tarqui got silently into the second jeep. Muhammed asked him if he was all right in Arabic, but the man wouldn't answer. His eyes were on the back of Zachary's head, and there was fear in his motionless face.

Elinor climbed in beside Zachary, ignoring Lillemor's annoyance and the fact that the other girl had obviously wanted to sit beside her cousin.

'These Tuareg scare me,' she said. 'I wish one could see what they're thinking.'

Zachary smiled gently. 'You're imagining things!' he taunted her.

'Well, you look out!' she replied, stealing a glance at the silent guide. 'He looks ready for anything to me!'

'You're prejudiced,' Zachary told her.

'Yes, I am,' she admitted. 'I'm sure they had something to do with——' She broke off, aware that Lillemor was listening to her open-mouthed.

'With what?' Zachary pressed her.

'With nothing,' she said with a sigh. It wasn't possible to talk to Zachary properly, so it was better to say nothing at all. But even if he wasn't going to watch the Tarqui, she was. Every inch of the way down south to the desert country where he came from.

The country became poorer as they went south. Elinor tried to pretend to herself that she was not stiff and urgently in need of a rest. She thought back to her father's anxious face as he had bidden them all goodbye. He had been annoyed that Zachary was going with them, but he had looked better, she thought. His colour had been more as she had remembered it in the past, and that had been such a relief to her that she had scarcely minded his aggressive tone to Zachary, or even his sharp-tongued questions to herself.

She stirred uncomfortably and was rewarded by a slight smile from Zachary.

'Are you sure we're going the right way?' Lillemor asked Gerard anxiously. 'We've seen nothing but a few palm trees and sand for miles!'

Gerard glanced at the compass he had fitted to the front of his jeep.

'I think so,' he said.

'Why don't we ask the guides?' Zachary drawled.

'We've left them too far behind!' Gerard retorted grimly.

Zachary shrugged his shoulders.

'If I were you, I'd wait for them to catch up. It will be dusk soon and we still have a long way to go.'

Gerard glared at him over his shoulder.

'If you can do so much better, why don't you drive for a bit?' he suggested crossly.

'Okay,' Zachary agreed calmly. 'If that's the way you want it. We're only a couple of miles out. There's a Tuareg encampment over on our left there.'

'Then why didn't you say so?' Gerard exploded with suppressed wrath.

'Oh, I don't know,' Zachary replied, at his most maddening. 'I guess you didn't ask me.'

Gerard pulled the wheel ferociously and they shot off at a tangent in the direction Zachary had indicated. From some way behind the two guides saw them change direction and adjusted their own course accordingly. With the change of direction there was a change in the direction of the wind and the sand blew up into their faces, burning their skins where it touched. Zachary pulled his turban further over his face, but even so Elinor could tell that he was smiling.

'I suppose you *did* see the encampment?' she asked him quietly.

'Too right I did!' he assured her cheerfully.

It was at that moment that the wheels began to sink into a sandbank. Gerard roared the engine, but they only sank lower until they came to a skidding halt. Zachary dropped lightly out of the jeep on to the sand and surveyed the half-hidden wheels.

'We'd better put down some canvas and push like mad,' he told them. 'If we wait for the guides, they can shove as well.'

They waited in a taut silence. Elinor knew that Gerard was blaming Zachary for their plight, sure that he had deliberately suggested that they should travel through the loose sand. Zachary, on the other hand, remained aloof from the whole business. If he thought anything, it was only that the driver should have been looking at the road ahead to forestall such an accident. Elinor shook her head at him, but he only laughed.

'In Australia we have an expression for this sort of thing,' he said. 'But with ladies present, I'd better not use it!'

Lillemor looked up and smiled. 'No, you'd better not!' She looked about her moodily. 'It's strange out here, isn't it?'

Zachary screwed up his eyes and peered into the distance.

'You get used to it,' he said abruptly. 'We're being watched.'

Elinor stared at the horizon, trying to see what he had seen, but she could see nothing at all but sand and the strong evening light that lit up the few palm-trees. The absence of anything human made her flesh creep.

'How do you know?' she asked.

Zachary glanced into the distance again. 'They're there. They look friendly enough. They might even come and help.'

He waited for the other jeep to come up to them, shouting to Muhammed to keep it out of the drift that they had landed up in.

'We're being watched,' he told the two men. 'Are they friendly?'

Ammamun, the Tarqui, shaded his eyes and looked around.

'They are my people,' he said reluctantly. He gave Zachary a peculiar but not unfriendly look. 'They are coming this way,' he added.

It was still some minutes before anyone else could see them. They came slowly, a group of Tuareg mounted on camels, their blue veils pulled tight up to just beneath their eyes. They sat on saddles that fitted the single hump of the animals they were riding, with their feet tucked comfortably into the beast's neck. When at last they arrived, they gathered round in silence and watched the strangers in the two jeeps. Finally their leader uttered a harsh order to his camel and the beast rocked down on to its knees and lay down on the sand for its master to dismount.

Ammamun hid his head behind the jeep and tried to ignore the arrival of the Tuareg. Zachary gave him a calculating look and stepped forward to greet the leader of the blue-veiled men.

'*Metulem, metulem,*' he said. He solemnly rubbed palms together with the leader and placed his hand on his heart, ending with the Arab salute of touching his fingers to his lips.

The leader looked round the little party.

'What brings you to the south again?' he asked Zachary.

'Justice,' Zachary smiled back at him.

'It is well.'

'*Insh-Allah,*' Zachary responded. 'God's will will be done.'

The leader strode round the jeep, looking at it from every angle. In doing so he caught sight of Ammamun.

'*Metulem!*' he cried in greeting, then the good will froze on his face. He turned curiously to Zachary, who was still at his side.

'You travel with your enemy?' he asked, astonished.

Zachary looked amused. He pulled a packet of cigarettes out of his pocket and offered the Tarqui one. The man took it with evident delight, turned his head modestly aside and deftly began to smoke it beneath his veil.

'An enemy defeated is an enemy no longer,' Zachary said easily. 'This one is of no account.'

Ammamun looked relieved. He went up to the leader then and exchanged lengthy greetings with him, inquiring after his father, his sons, his whole family, before finally coming to the point.

'It is true,' he said at last. 'It was I who betrayed Si

143

Zachary to serve the Caid. He would have died if it had not been so.'

'And you?' the leader asked him ironically.

'I lived in the desert for a long time,' Ammamun answered quietly. 'When I heard that Si Zachary was back in Meknes, I returned also to be a guide again.'

The leader looked at him long and hard.

'It will be best if you all make camp with us tonight,' he said at last. 'Our women will set up a tent for you and you can sleep soundly under our protection. In the morning,' he added to Zachary, 'if it is justice that you seek, I will ride with you. It was I who brought you south before and therefore it is I who will revenge you.'

The two men shook hands and hugged each other. Then Zachary caught Elinor by the hand and drew her forward.

'This is my wife,' he introduced her.

The leader shook hands with her too.

'And yet not your wife,' he said and, when Elinor blushed, looked almost as grimly satisfied as did Zachary.

CHAPTER ELEVEN

By way of revenge, Elinor pushed Lillemor forward to be introduced in her turn, but the Tarqui leader had already turned away and was busy signalling to his men to dismount and help push the jeep back on to its course. One by one, the stately camels rocked themselves down on to their knees and uttering fierce, unintelligible curses at their owners allowed them to dismount, while they surveyed the world with utter disdain.

Lillemor looked bewildered. 'What was that all about?' she asked.

'We're going to make camp with them,' Elinor explained briefly. 'It should be an interesting experience!'

Lillemor gave her a horrified look. 'Do you mean to tell me we're not stopping at some hotel?' the Australian girl demanded. 'What on earth are we going to eat? And as if we aren't tired enough without spending a sleepless night on the sand!'

Elinor giggled.

'I think it will be rather fun!' she exclaimed lightly. 'I've never done anything like it before.'

Lillemor groaned. 'We can be pretty hearty in Australia,' she complained. 'It's a mighty big country! But at least we take proper equipment with us!'

The men pushed and shoved without avail. In the end they had to lift the jeep bodily and set it down again on firmer sand.

'They'll go on ahead and tell their womenfolk that we're coming,' Zachary told Gerard. The Frenchman made no secret of his dislike for the arrangement. He hadn't even been consulted, and it was his expedition after all.

'Just what game are you playing?' he asked Zachary. 'I'm here to buy skins, and I won't have you mucking up my plans!'

Zachary shrugged his shoulders. 'I shan't interfere with you,' he promised. 'My being here will probably help you in the long run.'

'Pretty long run!' Gerard said bitterly. 'I can't think why Elinor had to invite you in the first place!'

'She didn't,' Zachary told him sweetly. 'It was my idea. I have unfinished business down here.'

'So it seems,' Gerard said dryly. 'You seem to know them all!'

'I had time to get to know most of them,' Zachary reminded him. 'Two years is a mighty long time.'

Gerard whistled under his breath. 'So you were here!' he said.

'Round about,' Zachary agreed. 'It took me some time to find a way out. Walking in this country is the equivalent of suicide.'

Gerard looked about him and shivered despite the heat.

'We'd better get started,' he said gruffly. 'Tell the girls to get in, will you?'

The Tuareg remounted their camels and swayed off ahead of them. Camels are curious animals; always appearing to stroll along, they cover the ground at an unexpectedly rapid rate. Gerard started up the jeep and gestured to Muhammed to do the same. Elinor jumped back into the jeep with a sigh. They hadn't far to go now, but the last few miles are always the worst when you are hot and tired and have been sitting in a car all day.

The Tuareg led the way with a confidence born of being bred in the desert. Remembering the vehicles coming behind them, they tested the sand as they went, picking their way round the outcrops of rock that showed here and there through the cover of sand and small stones.

'Oh, look!' Elinor breathed as they reached the brow of

146

the hill. 'Isn't that a beautiful sight!'

A silence fell over them as they looked down at the sight beyond them. A number of red tents, made redder still in the last rays of the sun, nestled into the valley and were surrounded by animals of all sorts, goats, camels and a number of scraggy dogs. There was no sign of water, as the Tuareg seldom camp anywhere near anyone else and find the waterholes overcrowded. Instead they carry every drop of water that they need, the children often travelling as much as twelve or fifteen miles to fill the goatskins for their mothers.

When they got nearer they could see that the tents were not very high. A man would have to stoop inside, but they were large enough to be really comfortable and for whole families to be able to spread themselves around.

'Is that where we're staying?' Lillemor asked. There was an undertone of excitement in her voice that was catching to the rest of them.

'That's it!' Gerard said with a smile.

The Tuareg rode their camels right into the camp and dismounted, calling out to their womenfolk to come and greet the strangers.

'*Metulem, metulem!*' they shouted eagerly. People came running out of every tent, to stop a few feet away from the jeeps and to stare silently at the strangers. The children up to the age of seven were all stark naked, but every boy over the age of thirteen wore the now familiar blue veil.

One of the women, who turned out to be the wife of the leader, came slowly forward and held out the palms of her hands in greeting.

'This is Takoma,' the leader introduced her in the indulgent tones of a man much in love with his wife. 'She will raise your tents for you.'

To Elinor, she looked too frail to manage such an undertaking on her own, but the woman herself didn't appear to be in the least bit daunted by the task. By making signs

147

with her hands, she asked the two girls where they wanted to be, pointing out the advantages and the disadvantages of the various sites. The men all gathered about the fires and left it to the women to do the work. Elinor longed to do likewise, but it didn't seem to be fair to leave all the labour to their hostesses, so she and Lillemor hung about and watched them work, incredulous at the rapid way they erected the shelters.

It was a pretty spectacle to watch. The women began by driving in the tent-pegs, carved out of tamarisk and gaily coloured to suit the fancy of some unknown artist. Then one of them knelt down to dig a hole for the pole, while another lowered in the forked pole, packing the sand around its base with her bare feet. When they were all upright, another pole was laid along the forks and the heavy roof was dragged across the top. Made of perhaps as many as twenty goatskins sewn together, it was dyed the same distinctive red as all the others. Lastly it was pulled tight, but it no-where touched the ground, as in the full heat of the day it would have been unbearably hot.

Lastly the women brought a pile of mats, which not only covered the floor but also served as moveable walls, that could be rolled up at will. They were made of woven reeds and edged with leather and in their way were extremely handsome articles.

When they had finished the girls' tent, they started on one for the two men. Muhammed and Ammamun would curl up in their cloaks under the sky, close to the embers of the fire for warmth. Elinor wondered how the two men would get along together at such close quarters, then thought wryly that she would probably do better to worry about how she was going to get on with Lillemor. She went to the jeep and gathered together her possessions, dumping them into the tent that she and Lillemor were to share. When she had done, she returned to the fire and sat down beside the men.

Zachary looked up at her arrival.

'They're going to put on the equivalent of an *ahal* for us this evening,' he told her. 'You'll have to dress up in your best bib and tucker!'

Elinor laughed. 'What's an *ahal*?' she asked.

Zachary squinted at the fire. 'It's a kind of dance,' he explained. 'The Tuareg are a matriarchy of sorts and it's the women who choose their own husbands. They look the young men over and make their choice. Tonight, however, they're only going to sing and dance for us!'

She grinned. 'Then I shall have to wear my very best,' she agreed. 'Necklace and all!'

For a moment she thought he was going to forbid her to do any such thing, but slowly his expression relaxed.

'If you want to,' he said. 'I'm not stopping you.'

Gerard looked across at the two of them.

'Must you?' he asked them. 'Do you have to bicker all the time?'

Zachary laughed. 'All women like to exercise their tongues!' he retorted. 'Why don't you keep her entertained for me, then I wouldn't have to bother?'

The stormy look on Gerard's face was mirrored in Elinor's.

'I'm sorry if I've been boring you!' she exclaimed, hurt. She drew away from him and went to sit on the other side of the fire beside Gerard. No sooner had she moved than Lillemor slipped into the place she had just vacated.

'Not at all,' said Zachary ironically.

It was hard to leave the fire and go into the cold tent to change. As soon as the sun had set, the cold had begun to grip the sand. The dramatic change of temperature made it seem colder than it really was, and every little wind that blew the fine dust about the desert added to the illusion.

'What do you intend to wear?' Lillemor asked wearily. The long day had taken a toll from her beauty and there were dark smudges beneath her eyes and a downward tilt to her mouth that spoke silently of her complete exhaustion.

'The most colourful dress I have,' Elinor answered. 'I brought it specially. Only very bright colours show up well in firelight.'

Lillemor flung herself down on the pile of mats.

'Frankly I don't care!' she said. 'All I know is that I could sleep for a week!'

Elinor smiled sympathetically. 'The coolness of the night will wake you up. And the food! All I could see to eat was goat's milk!'

'No?' Lillemor said, revolted. 'Oh no! I saw a sack of millet somewhere.'

Elinor opened up her suitcase and delved inside it for her dress and cosmetics.

'That's good,' she said with satisfaction. 'It sounds like *couscous*!'

Lillemor grunted and rolled over to look at what the other girl was doing.

'Again?' she said bleakly.

Elinor giggled. 'Don't you like it?'

But Lillemor didn't answer. Elinor cast her a searching look to make sure that she was all right, but the other girl merely looked tired from the long drive south.

'Would you like a drink?' she asked her. 'Both the men brought a flask of something, and I don't suppose it's water.'

'I think I would,' Lillemor agreed with surprising meekness. 'I'm all right. I'm just tired.'

She hoisted herself to her feet and hit her head on the skin roofing of the tent. Making a face of distaste and discomfort, she began searching in her own luggage for something to wear.

'And Zachary thinks this is fun!' she muttered.

'So it is!' Elinor exclaimed. 'I wouldn't have missed it for anything!'

Lillemor made a small gesture of despair.

'Then one of us is stark, staring mad!' she said.

Elinor thought she had never seen a more beautiful sight than the encampment by moonlight. The cooking fires lit up little patches of the desert, casting peculiar shadows over the white sand. The outcrops of rock looked strange and sinister and a romantic thrall held the whole area, so that it didn't seem to be quite real. In the centre was the main fire and a couple of old hurricane lamps that cast their own smoky, flickering light. It was here that the men sat, their blue *lithams* black in the darkness so that all one could see of them were the whites of their eyes in a black shape. The women were still busy, cooking and making the camp secure for the night. Their jewellery flashed in the firelight, jangling gaily as they walked about.

Elinor fingered her own necklace. She wore it proudly, pleased that she had something that they would know and recognise. When she came out of her tent, though, she could feel Zachary's eyes burning into her and she tried to ignore him. Why shouldn't she wear it? she thought. For an instant she nearly turned round to put it back inside her tent, but at that moment the wife of the leader, Takoma, caught her by the hand and dragged her nearer to the fire.

Takoma spoke French and she could read and write better than her husband. It was odd to find that the women were the guardians of learning and culture so deep in the desert and in a country where their sisters more often than not had no education and no rights at all in their family, not even the right to be counted as a person when the census of many country towns was taken.

'What is the matter with your friend?' Takoma asked, stumbling a little over the unaccustomed words.

'She is tired,' Elinor answered. 'We have come a long way today.'

Takoma nodded. Her own body was well able to withstand any demands that she cared to make on it. She would often walk twenty miles in a day for no other reason than that she wanted to visit with a friend. She glanced across at Lillemor, a puzzled look on her face, but she said nothing; she was far too intent on finding out all she could about the whole party.

Elinor found herself telling her all about her life in Morocco as a child and later of her nursing in England. When she had done she was a little ashamed of herself for speaking so freely. She had told Takoma more than she had ever told another living soul about her feelings in the last few years.

'I should talk less and let you get on with entertaining your other guests!' she ended with a shy smile.

Takoma laughed. 'It is good to speak sometimes,' she said lightly. She put out an inquisitive hand and fingered Elinor's necklace. 'Where did you get this?' she asked.

Elinor tried to read the Tarqui woman's mind, to know what she was thinking, but Takoma's face was completely enigmatic.

'Si Zachary gave it to me,' she answered cautiously.

'It is Chleuh!' Takoma exclaimed.

Elinor nodded. 'It's pretty, don't you think?' she commented.

But Takoma shook her head. 'It is not lucky!' she said.

'Why not?' Elinor demanded.

Takoma dropped it sharply so that it landed with a dull thud against Elinor's neck. It felt suddenly cold and foreign to her.

'What does it mean?' she asked passionately.

Takoma's eyes grew large with superstitious fear.

'It has the sign of a man upon it,' she answered reluctantly. 'An evil man. He is not your friend and he is the sworn enemy of Si Zachary. While you wear his mark you are in bondage to him!'

Elinor tried to dismiss the words as being nothing more

than the fear of a primitive people for the written word.

'He cannot harm us!' she scoffed.

But Takoma nodded her head violently.

'He has already harmed Si Zachary. He will again if he has the opportunity. You must take off the necklace! It is unlucky for you!'

Elinor tried to tell herself that it was to please the Tarqui woman that she took it off and put it back in her tent, but it wasn't altogether. She too was afraid, so afraid that she could almost feel the strength of some man's grasp within the necklace. She could laugh at herself for allowing herself to be influenced by such a ridiculous idea, but the feeling was still there with her and she was glad to be rid of the necklace and to return to the fire without it.

In the incredible way that news travels in the Sahara, people from afar had learned that strangers had come south to visit the Tuareg. All through the evening their numbers expanded as yet more men came into the encampment on their camels, bringing in the hides they were willing to trade for salt and millet. No matter how far the distance they had come their eyes lit up when they saw the party in progress and, one and all, they leaped off their camels and immediately joined in the dancing and feasting.

Mostly the women would sing. One of them would take up the *imzad*, the single-stringed Tarqui guitar, and begin to sing. Sooner or later one of the men would begin to drum away on a piece of stretched goatskin and the concert would have started in earnest. Occasionally two of the men would dance out the movements of a battle, with their heavy and distinctive swords and their shields made of giraffe skin, usually rather badly cured because their lives no longer depended on them. It was a long time since the Tuareg had set out to trap a passing caravan, or to exact tribute from an unwilling vassal tribe. None of these men had ever taken part in battle themselves, but the stories they told were none the less vivid for having happened to their fathers and grandfathers.

Elinor sat on a hump of rocks and watched until her eyelids were heavy and the fires had burned down low. She would have been completely happy had she not known that Zachary and Lillemor were sitting just beyond the circle of the Tuareg, talking in undertones to one another, as if they alone shared all the secrets of the night. Every now and again she could hear Lillemor's laugh ring out and she could hear Zachary telling stories, his accent becoming more and more Australian as the evening wore on. Elinor played with her fingers in the sand and was surprised when they met with something hard and crystal shaped. When she picked it up and looked at it, she saw that the sand had crystallised into the shape of a flower of many petals. She fingered it gently, wondering how it had come to be. She hated Zachary, she decided bleakly. She hated him and she hated Lillemor too!

'Look!' she said to Gerard. She held out the crystallised sand to him and placed it in his open palm.

'Where did you find it?' he asked her.

'Just here.' She felt about with her hands to see if there were any more, but it was all dry and dusty and there was nothing to see. 'I suppose it must have been caused by rain,' she mused. 'Isn't it perfectly shaped?'

Gerard smiled.

'It's a sand rose. Occasionally you can see them for sale in the towns. Tourists love to buy them!'

Elinor laughed. 'This one is different,' she decided. 'I found it for myself, so no one can accuse me of cheating, can they?'

'No,' he agreed. 'I shall be your witness to my dying day!'

He came and sat a little closer, sharing the same outcrop of stones for a seat.

'Elinor, are you glad you came?' he asked suddenly.

154

Elinor hesitated. 'I think so. Will you get all the skins you need?'

'If Zachary doesn't interfere with the sale. Why did he come? Do you know?'

Elinor shook her head. 'I'm beginning to think that I may have guessed,' she said. 'Do you think he could have spent those two years down here among the Tuareg?'

Gerard shrugged his shoulders. 'It doesn't seem very likely. The government were looking for him for a long time. I should have thought they would have found him here.'

'But the Tuareg are mostly in Algeria, aren't they? Didn't they at one time rule Northern Nigeria as well? They come and go as they like, across frontiers and back again.'

'Maybe,' Gerard agreed. He didn't seem to be very impressed with the idea. 'These ones are friendly enough, anyway,' he said.

'Yes. But they all know something. They know him well and they share his secret. I wish he'd tell us and have done!'

'Typical!' Gerard agreed with contempt. 'I think he likes being the centre of everyone's attention. Anyone else would have given some explanation long ago!'

'Perhaps,' Elinor said gently. 'I really don't know!' she added on a sigh. 'You should have seen his back!'

Gerard looked vaguely uncomfortable.

'I suppose,' he said after a long pause, 'you haven't thought any more about us. You can't go on like this, neither one thing nor the other—and nor can I!'

Elinor turned her back on him and prodded thoughtfully at the sand.

'I won't be hurried, Gerard,' she said finally. 'This time I'm going to be *sure* before I do anything at all!' She stood up in an unhurried movement and smiled down at him. 'Why don't you try your luck with Lillemor?' she suggested almost hopefully. 'You shouldn't let Zachary completely monopolise her, you know.'

Gerard rose too.

'All right,' he said sourly. 'Your wish is my command! But remember that it's *at* your command!'

Elinor chuckled. 'I will,' she said.

Gerard was more successful than she had hoped. He offered to show Lillemor how to play the Tarqui guitar and in a few minutes she had got the hang of the thing and, to the intense joy of the Tuareg, she obliged by singing them some of the old songs from Australia, songs about the bush and the gold rush that had once caught the entire population in their grip.

Left alone, Zachary came strolling over to Elinor.

'That was a very successful manoeuvre,' he congratulated her.

She looked up at him innocently. 'What are you talking about?' she asked.

He grinned, his teeth showing white in the darkness.

'As if you really didn't know!' he mocked her. He held out his hand to her and pulled her to her feet. 'Have you had enough of the song and dance?' he asked her, almost uncertainly as if he couldn't be sure what her answer would be. 'Will you come for a stroll in the desert?'

'I'd love to,' she said frankly. 'It's beautiful, isn't it?'

He didn't let go her hand and she didn't like to pull it away from him, though she was absurdly conscious of the contact. He was an easy person to walk with, she thought. Their steps matched, or at least he shortened his to meet hers, and they both appeared to want to go in the same direction, away from the camp towards a lengthy plain that stretched away to the next rise of hills, and the next, and the next.

They walked on until the fires were no more than points of light, surrounded by black shadows that moved in time to the music. The music would carry through the desert for miles, the endless Saharan rhythm beating against the rocks and the sand and only faintly distorted by the occasional palm trees that grew in groups wherever there was water to be had.

Elinor kept a close watch on where her feet were going because she was a little afraid of scorpions, or some other terror of the desert, even though she didn't know what these dread animals could be. She was the first to notice, therefore, the curious bed of sand that had been built up by the hands of man and was now deserted, to be picked away by the sudden gusts of wind.

'What's this?' she asked, immediately curious.

Zachary smiled and kicked at the sand with his foot.

'It's a marriage bed,' he told her.

'Right out here?'

'It's within sight of the camp,' he answered. 'When the Tuareg marry, they spend days going through the various ceremonies. On their wedding night they make this bed of sand and then the day after they move their tent to another site. The longer the bed holds out against the wind, the happier their marriage will be.'

Elinor stared down at the sand, half embarrassed and half sad.

'Ours must have blown away in the first storm that touched it,' she said. She could feel Zachary's eyes on her, but she wouldn't return his look.

'Perhaps,' he said. 'Perhaps it's still there—underneath.'

She shook her head without saying anything.

'We'll find out,' he promised her. 'We'll find out just as soon as I've finished things down here.'

'Must you?' she begged of him. 'It might be dangerous!'

'Down here?' He laughed. 'There's no need to worry, my dear. *This time* I know what I'm doing!'

But the magic had gone out of the evening. Elinor turned to go back to the camp and he fell in beside her, as silent as he had been before. Elinor glanced across at the camp and was surprised to notice that people were still coming into the camp. The small black figures swaying gently on their camels were a sight to behold in the moonlight.

'There's someone important arriving now,' she pointed out. 'Look! Practically everyone has got up to greet him!'

Zachary screwed up his eyes to see if he could make out the new arrival.

'Ah,' he said with satisfaction. 'This is what I've been waiting for. Do you mind if we run?'

Elinor thought she had never moved so fast. Zachary rushed over the ground, half dragging her with him. He meant to be in at the beginning of the greetings for this latest arrival. In the moonlight she could see the tense, absorbed expression on his face and she began to be afraid. Was this the man whom he had come to see? The man, perhaps, who had held him captive? Who might even have administered that beating which had left his back raw and bleeding?

'Who is this man?' she gasped.

'The Caid of El Hammam!'

They gained the camp just as the first of the camels lurched to its knees to allow its rider to dismount. Elinor saw the faint glitter of excitement in Zachary's eyes. She wanted to rush forward and tell the Caid to mount up again and go on his way before there was any trouble, but that wouldn't have suited Zachary at all. She was surprised to see him step forward and personally help the old man to dismount. Above his *litham*, Elinor could see the look of astonishment in the old man's eyes. It was almost as if he were seeing a ghost.

'You!' he exclaimed in a peculiar cracked voice.

Zachary's teeth showed white and strong.

'Yes, it is I!' he agreed in Arabic. 'As you can see, Allah was with me!'

CHAPTER TWELVE

The silence in the camp was almost tangible. Elinor looked round the silent watchful faces of the Tuareg and wondered at Zachary's boldness. Whatever they had expected, it had certainly not been this respectful, almost filial gesture on Zachary's part.

Zachary himself seemed blissfully unaware that anyone was watching him.

'I thought you would come when you heard that some English people had come looking for skins,' he said in Arabic. 'They might have had news of me, isn't that right?'

The old man nodded. 'I was sure you were dead!' he replied in the same unbelieving tones.

Zachary looked suddenly stern. 'I could well have been!' The unyielding menace behind his words made Elinor blink.

'What are you planning to do?' she asked him in English. She felt uncomfortable in such an atmosphere and she had never seen Zachary look so hard and dangerous.

'I plan to see that he is punished!' he retorted. He said it so pleasantly that she could hardly believe that he really meant it.

'How?'

He frowned at her. 'I'll find a way. He's scared now!'

Elinor shivered. 'So am I! Zachary, it won't be dangerous, will it?'

Zachary looked deep into the old man's eyes.

'I hope not!' he said smoothly.

Elinor looked for support from Lillemor and Gerard, but neither of them was in sight. It was hard to know what to do. She was uncomfortably aware that the fear in the Caid's eyes was reflected in her own and in the silence of everybody else. Only Zachary was calm and smiling.

'I hope you will be comfortable for the night?' he said to the old man. 'Shall I see about the erection of a tent for you?'

The Caid shook his head. 'I shall sleep with my men around the fire,' he answered.

Zachary smiled again and bowed. 'Let us hope you will be blessed with the sleep of the innocent!' he said piously.

The old man started, but he said nothing more. He made a sign with his hand and his men moved in close beside him. Zachary watched them through narrowed eyes, then he turned away and ignored them as thoroughly as if they were no longer there.

'You look tired too,' he said gently to Elinor. 'It looks as if Lillemor has already gone to bed. If I were you I should join her.'

Elinor nodded. There was nothing else she could do. One by one the Tuareg had recovered from their fright and were settling down for the night, detaching themselves from the group that surrounded the fire and making their way to their tents and their beds.

'Goodnight,' she said.

'Goodnight,' he answered her, so softly his words were almost a caress. 'I'll walk you to your tent.'

Lillemor had pulled down all the mats so the tent was in darkness when Elinor entered. She laid out her sleeping bag on a thick pile of mats and undressed as rapidly as she could in the darkness, climbing into her pyjamas and then wriggling down into the warmth of the sleeping bag.

'Are you asleep?' she whispered across to Lillemor, but the Australian didn't answer. Elinor could hear her shuffling as she turned over, but whether she was awake or not she couldn't tell.

She herself was too excited to sleep. The atmosphere in the tent, roomy as it was, seemed oppressive and she longed for a breath of the cool air of the night. The goatskins above her smelt and so did the mats beneath her. Even her sleeping bag, it was so long since she had used it, was constricting and prevented her from moving about freely. She had almost forgotten the art of taking the bedclothes with her as a kind of outer skin and every time she moved she seemed to get into a worse muddle and was hotter than ever. In the end she rolled up the mat beside her that was forming part of the wall and lay there, gazing out at the dying embers of the fire and the sleeping forms of the men around it.

The moon shone brightly on her face and the stars seemed bigger and more brilliant than they ever did in England. She supposed it was because of the fineness of the atmosphere over the desert and wished idly that she knew more about the stars and could tell at a glance one group from another as some people could.

She must have slept, for when she next woke the moon had crossed the skies and she was lying in complete darkness. It was the other side of the tents that was being lit up now and she could see them clearly, fantastic silhouettes against the rocky sand. She awoke with a start and was wide awake immediately. Something must have moved and startled her, for she could feel the tenseness of the muscles all down her legs, although she was completely unaware of what it was that had disturbed her.

She lay in silence and listened and watched. For a long time there was nothing and then she saw a shadow creeping towards the tent that Zachary and Gerard were sharing. Elinor caught her breath and the gasping noise she made seemed to cross the open space with unbelievable clarity. And yet nobody had heard her, for the silent shadow never altered his pace, or glanced around to see who was watching him.

Elinor wriggled out of her bag and through the gap between the goatskin roof of the tent and the ground. The sand struck coldly on her feet as she crept across the space between the two tents. She was frightened and could hear her own heartbeats thudding in her head, but she was even more frightened for the sleeping Zachary. Supposing someone was to catch him unawares, or worse, to murder him as he lay there sleeping? A hundred alternatives spun through her brain in a matter of seconds, and then she had reached the tent and there was no one to be seen.

Anxiously she looked about her. She forgot her former caution and stood right out in the moonlight, searching the shadows with her eyes, but there was nothing. With a rising sense of panic she tore at the mat that formed the entrance to Zachary's tent. It made a light rustling noise as she moved it. Distraught, she pushed her way underneath it and fell on to the nearest sleeping-bag. A hand gripped her arm in a vice that bruised her flesh.

'What the devil——?' Zachary exclaimed.

Elinor rubbed at her arm, beginning to wonder herself exactly what she was doing.

'A man——' she began in a whisper she could only just hear herself. 'I could see his shadow coming towards the tent!'

Zachary freed himself from his sleeping bag with a single competent movement. He pulled her up on to her feet beside him and whispered softly back.

'Stay here and *don't* move!'

She watched him move silently out of the tent and waited for as long as she could bear to, and then, as she could still hear nothing, she began to follow him to see what was happening. He was standing just outside the entrance to the tent and she very nearly banged into him, but he saw her in time and gave her a hard push back into the tent. Elinor tripped and fell heavily across Gerard's prone body. He stirred sleepily and yawned practically into her face.

'*Qu'est-ce qu'il y a?*' he began. 'Good heavens! What on earth are you doing?'

Elinor got uneasily to her feet. 'There's an intruder outside,' she muttered.

'There's one inside!' Gerard retorted in a shocked voice. 'Where's Zachary?'

'Outside!' Elinor almost snapped at him.

'Perhaps I'd better see——' he began vaguely.

'No, don't! *I* shall go and see,' she said firmly. 'Though with all this noise going on I don't suppose there'll be anything to see!'

Gerard wound himself back into his bedclothes.

'Sorry,' he said. 'You'd do far better to go back to bed!' he added with irritated concern. 'Zachary can look after himself!'

Elinor crept out of the tent again, more than a little annoyed by the encounter. She was beginning to think that she must have imagined the whole affair and that she would have done a great deal better to have gone back to sleep as easily and with the same lack of curiosity that Gerard had. Zachary was still standing in the shadows of the tent, and then, beyond him, deeper in the shadows, she saw something move again. In a flash, Zachary had jumped and there was a soft gurgling sound as he toppled the man to the ground.

'There's a torch in the jeep,' he told her. His voice sounded very loud in the stillness of the night, making her jump. She hurried across to the jeep and came back with the torch, shining it down on the unknown man. His blue veil had slipped a little and he struggled to pull it up, ashamed of any woman seeing his face. But it was not his face that Elinor saw. Round his neck he wore a necklace that was identical in every respect to the one that Zachary had given her.

Zachary slowly released the man, keeping a watchful eye on him for any move to escape.

'Look!' breathed Elinor. 'Look at that necklace!'

Zachary grinned. He reached out a hand and pulled the

necklace off the man's neck.

'A servant of the Caid, no less!' he commented.

The man began to speak passionately in his own language. Zachary listened in silence.

'He says,' he said at last, 'that he was told to keep an eye on me, that was all. The Caid is afraid that I may bring in the police and his activities wouldn't bear their interest. I'll say not!'

'And are you?' Elinor asked. Her fright had caught up with her and she felt weak at the knees and decidedly frail.

'No,' he said slowly. 'The old man isn't a bad taskmaster by his own lights.'

'How can you say that?' Elinor demanded fiercely. 'When I think about your back——'

He put an arm about her shoulders and held her close.

'Don't!' he whispered. 'That's all in the past!'

She was comforted and was warmed by his closeness.

'I wish I could believe it,' she sighed.

Zachary spoke to the man once again and the man nodded his consent. He went over to his friends and disappeared among their reclining shadows. In a matter of seconds he too appeared to be sleeping.

'You must go back to bed too,' Zachary whispered to Elinor. 'We shan't have any more trouble tonight.'

He walked her slowly to the entrance to her tent and watched as she folded up the mat and went inside. As she climbed back into her sleeping bag, she could hear his footsteps as he went back to his own tent. The warmth of the bag surrounded her body and she realised just how tired she was. In a matter of seconds she was sound asleep.

The first stirrings in the camp were at dawn. The Tuareg symbolically washed their hands in sand because there was so little water and bowed down to Mecca in the first prayer of the day. Elinor rolled over sleepily, protesting as she did so at the idea of having to get up.

'I'm stiff!' she moaned.

Lillemor leaned up on her elbow and looked at her.

'What was going on last night?' she asked. There was a dangerous look in her eyes and her mouth was pulled down at the edges showing her complete displeasure.

'There was a man keeping watch on Zachary,' Elinor explained. 'I thought he might be going to hurt him.'

Lillemor's eyes narrowed.

'I didn't mean then! I meant earlier. I thought you'd given up your claim to Zachary? Isn't it time you began to realise that you're strictly his *ex*-wife? I suppose you thought I wouldn't notice if you went off walking with him!'

Elinor yawned. 'I can't say I thought about it at all!' she said slowly. 'Does it matter?'

'It matters to me!' Lillemor assured her sullenly. 'I want Zachary for myself. That's why I came to Morocco. I never believed he was dead. I meant to find him and take him back to Australia with me!'

'I don't think he'd go,' Elinor said reasonably. She didn't want to hear Lillemor's plans for the future! Not if they concerned Zachary! She rolled over in her sleeping bag and examined closely the pattern of the mat that lay just beneath her head. The trouble was that she was hotly jealous of the Australian girl and she didn't want to admit it.

'What time is it?' Lillemor asked after a long silence.

Elinor glanced at her watch.

'Just after six. I suppose we'd better get started or the men will be wanting breakfast before we're ready for them!'

Lillemor stuck her head out of the tent and looked around.

'Gerard is lighting the brazier now,' she reported. 'If we waited long enough he might bring us breakfast in bed!'

Elinor grinned. 'He might! But I think I'll go and help him all the same. Coming?'

Lillemor shook her head. 'By my standards,' she said, 'this is the middle of the night. I'm going back to sleep again.'

It wasn't easy to get dressed when one was bent almost double avoiding the low roof. Elinor pulled on her clothing as quickly as she could, attending to her face first with a cleansing cream and then with her ordinary, everyday make-up. She rolled up her bed and packed her possessions neatly away inside her case. When she had finished, she rolled up the mat that formed the door of the tent, fastening it with a piece of string. Lillemor had humped herself back into her sleeping bag and was apparently asleep again. Elinor hesitated a second, wondering whether to say anything further, but the Australian girl's back looked completely unresponsive. It was a pity, she thought, because in any other circumstances she could have liked Lillemor very much indeed. It was only Zachary who kept coming between them, making it impossible for them to be friends.

Elinor slipped out of the tent as silently as she could. It was cold outside, for the sun had done no more than creep up to the horizon, flooding the sky with a pink and yellow light that changed every minute, from grey and green to the rich blue of the full day.

'Good morning,' Gerard grunted as she approached him.

Elinor squatted down beside him. 'Good morning,' she replied. 'How's it going?'

He almost looked at her, but not quite, his eyes sliding away from her face.

'Did you get what you wanted last night?' he asked.

'We caught the man, if that's what you mean?' Elinor replied.

'Then there really was a man?' he went on.

'Of course there was a man! Do you think I run around in my bare feet at night for fun?'

Again he almost looked at her.

'Elinor,' he said urgently, 'you must make up your mind!

166

It isn't right for you to go on as you have been doing! Why won't you agree to marry me? We could arrange everything as soon as we get home and there would be no more trouble—no more fuss! You would be free of him for ever!'

Elinor shook her head sadly.

'I'm fond of you, Gerard. Too fond of you to muddle up your life any further. I know you think you're in love with me, but you're not really. You don't even trust me, do you? You think I've been flighty in the past and there's always the danger that I may be again. Isn't that it, when you really think about it?'

He looked at her then. His startled face made her want to laugh and, because she knew she couldn't, she bit her lip instead.

'I think you got carried away when you married Zachary!' he answered her. 'It was so unlike you to do anything so rash! I can't think what your father was doing to allow it! It's quite obvious that it was a kind of mad infatuation—Zachary is just the right type to inspire that sort of thing!' he added not without bitterness.

Elinor smiled gently.

'For an infatuation, it's lasted a mighty long time!' she sighed.

Gerard poked at the few coals in the brazier.

'If you're trying to tell me that you're still in love with the fellow, I shan't believe you!' he said stoutly. 'Only look at the stupid game he's trying to play down here! He'd better see that he doesn't do anything to queer my pitch!'

Somehow the cricketing metaphor from a Frenchman was too much for Elinor. She burst openly into delighted laughter and once she had started she couldn't stop. She was still laughing when Zachary came over to join them.

'How's breakfast doing?' he asked.

Elinor tried to pull herself together. She picked up the frying pan that Gerard had brought across with him and placed it on the brazier. They had brought a few eggs and some salted meat with them and she prepared it now, heating up some of the millet that they had failed to eat the night before. It made a great pile of food, but the three of them tucked into it with a will. When it gets into the hundreds at midday no one wants a large meal at lunchtime.

The Tuareg women were milking their goats and they brought some of the milk for them to drink. Elinor, who never found it very palatable at any time, found it even nastier when warm and fresh, but she sipped a little of it so as not to offend them. Only Zachary seemed to truly welcome the gesture, but then he could eat their rancid butter with apparent pleasure as well, so perhaps he had some secret means of swallowing unpleasant things.

'What time are you holding your sale?' he asked Gerard.

Gerard flushed, naïvely pleased at being consulted.

'Before it gets too hot,' he answered.

'Good!' said Zachary. 'See that they all crowd round and listen, won't you? Especially the Caid and his party.' He laughed without much humour. 'I should imagine that they can offer you some particularly fine skins!'

Elinor said nothing. She went on eating her breakfast, but it seemed suddenly tasteless. She wished urgently that she really knew what it was that Zachary had at the back of his mind.

'I'd better take Lillemor her breakfast,' she said abruptly.

Zachary grinned. 'Put this on her tray,' he suggested, and handed her a piece of highly coloured Tuareg braiding that he had twisted into an elaborate bow. 'It may cheer her up!'

Elinor almost snatched it from him. She knew exactly what Lillemor would read into such a gesture and she couldn't help thinking that Zachary knew as well. Wishful thinking was hardly the prerogative of only one sex!

'If you wish,' she said coldly.

Zachary's grin grew broader.

'Oh, I do!' he said.

The Tuareg found the sale immensely exciting. They formed themselves into an enormous semi-circle around Gerard, sitting on their haunches and watching one another in an uncomfortable silence. The women stood further back, not taking any part in the proceedings, but with their interest showing in the tense excitement on their faces. But, for the moment, Elinor was only interested in the Caid. He sat on a small leather seat, completely surrounded by his followers. They all, without exception, wore identical necklaces under their shirts, similar to the one that Zachary had given her, and they all had their eyes fixed on Zachary.

Gerard called to Ammamun and through him began to talk about the skins he wished to buy. If, he suggested, they would place their own skins in individual piles, he would go round and offer them each a price for their own skins. The Tuareg nodded their approval. They rose silently and went to collect their skins, laying them out in front of them so that they could be seen to the best advantage. Gerard and Ammamun went slowly from group to group, looking at each skin and running their hands over it to see how well it had been prepared. Elinor could tell from the excitement on Gerard's face that they were good ones—very good indeed, and she was glad for him that his trip hadn't been wasted. He didn't seem to need any help from her, however, and she soon became bored of watching him repeat the same process over and over again, and her interest reverted to the Caid.

He sat quite still on his leather stool, occasionally throwing out a comment to one of his men. In front of him, the ground lay carpeted with his finest skins, all of excellent quality and laid out in sizes to save Gerard's time. At first sight he looked calm and very dignified. It was only when she had been watching him for several minutes that Elinor became aware that he too was watching Zachary.

At last it seemed that he couldn't bear it any longer. He held up an imperious finger and the nearest heads of his men bent towards him to find out his pleasure.

'I wondered how long he would last out,' Zachary commented, without appearing to speak at all.

Elinor jumped. 'I wish you wouldn't *creep* about!' she complained irritably.

Zachary whistled softly through his teeth.

'They'll be coming over for a parley in a few minutes,' he said. 'You wait and see!'

Elinor glanced at him anxiously.

'Zachary, you are sure you know what you're doing, aren't you?'

He threw her a quick smile. 'Too right I do! I've got him really worried. He was expecting me to threaten him, or to fight, but certainly not to do nothing! He'll agree to talk in a minute and then it will all be over.'

The Caid's men came slowly over. It was obvious that they didn't greatly relish the task he had given them.

'The Caid would like you to drink tea with him,' they said to Zachary.

Zachary's eyebrows rose a little at the ungracious way the invitation had been delivered.

'I think this is it,' he said to Elinor. 'Want to come along?'

Elinor nodded. Nothing would have kept her away. She looked quickly round the group of Tuareg and was surprised to see Lillemor already standing in the little group around the Caid.

'Why don't you go and look out for Gerard?' she whispered to Elinor. '*I* am staying with Zachary!'

Elinor forced herself to smile.

'Gerard is busy,' she replied calmly. 'Besides, the Caid is about to serve tea.'

The Caid, however, chose to ignore both girls as being unworthy of the tea ceremony. He motioned to Zachary to sit down beside him and told his servants to bring the tea tray. When it was brought, he spent a minute or so admiring his own silver and then he carefully made the tea and handed the first of the glasses to Zachary.

Punctiliously, both men swallowed down the requisite three glasses of the sweet, minty liquid, making polite conversation as they did so. Then as Zachary dropped his empty glass back on the tray, the Caid became more serious.

'Si Zachary,' he began uneasily, 'I have done you an injury and I admit it!'

Zachary looked up and smiled.

'You admit it?' he repeated lazily.

The Caid shrugged. 'I have no choice,' he said frankly. 'When I first sent for you I had urgent need of a doctor. I sent a man of the Chleuh to Meknes to fetch you and you cured me. It seemed a good thing to me to always have a doctor among my people. Why, I asked myself, should you return to the city?'

'And so you deliberately deprived me of my freedom,' Zachary prompted him.

The Caid nodded gravely.

'It seemed a small thing. You would never walk away from my tents, I assured myself, and there would be no more sickness among us.' He smiled with sudden charm at Zachary. 'But you were to walk into the desert not once, but twice!'

Zachary's eyes hardened at the memory.

'I suppose you thought that after the first time I would never attempt it again?' he said dryly.

Elinor gasped. She had found the whole conversation difficult to follow and, she was ashamed to admit to herself, if Lillemor had not been there, she would have long ago given up the pretence of being able to follow it. But this last she had understood!

171

'You mean that it was *he* who did that to your back?' she exploded into indignant English.

Zachary chuckled. He translated her remark for the Caid's benefit and the old man looked pained.

'It was not I!' he denied. 'It was one of my men,' he added indifferently. He smiled his singularly charming smile once again. 'I suppose you have come seeking justice. Compensation for those two years of your life?' He considered for a moment. 'I will pay you the price of these skins,' he said. 'Then the debt will be wiped out between us!'

Zachary rose to his feet and examined the skins with care. When he had done, he offered his hand to the Caid.

'It is very generous compensation,' he agreed.

Elinor could feel the tension seeping out of the air as even the Tuareg began to relax their watchfulness.

'You really are going to accept his offer, aren't you?' she asked Zachary in English.

'Yes, I am,' said Zachary. He grinned right into her eyes and then, suddenly, bent forward and kissed her full on the lips. 'And that's for caring!' he laughed at her.

Elinor blushed, bitterly aware of Lillemor's angry eyes on her.

'I—I never said I didn't!' she said weakly.

CHAPTER THIRTEEN

THE long drive back to Meknes proved far more wearing than the one which had brought them south. Elinor spent most of it trying to sleep. There had been little time for that the previous night. The Tuareg had been overjoyed at the sudden reconciliation between Zachary and the Caid. They had been afraid that the police would come and disturb the even tenor of their life, upsetting their own ideas of desert justice. But the fact that Zachary had been prepared to accept compensation just as one of them would have done was a matter for great celebrations. The party of the night before had paled into insignificance besides the dancing and merriment that began as soon as the sun went down.

Gerard, in a particularly good mood because the skins he had bought were so much finer than he had expected, agreed that they should split up and travel back in pairs, two to each jeep. The guides, he said, could travel as they wished. It was the skins he was concerned about. They had to be properly secured and properly folded so that none of them came to any harm.

Lillemor had gone with Zachary as a matter of course. Her air of triumph had travelled with Elinor for a great deal further than the first hundred miles of the journey. For some reason she couldn't get the slight smile out of her mind no matter how hard she tried. Gerard seemed a poor substitute to her and although she tried to be pleasant and friendly, she knew she was really being thoroughly crotchety and difficult.

'This heat barely allows one to think at all!' she complained, wiping the sweat off her face.

Gerard refused to be cast down.

173

'It was a pretty good party, though, don't you think?'

Elinor thought of Zachary dancing with Lillemor.

'I don't know,' she said wearily. 'I was too glad to know that Zachary was safe to care!'

Gerard looked at her suspiciously.

'What's the matter, dear?' he said at last.

The kindness in his voice undermined Elinor's defences and she wept unashamedly.

'He's only pleased to see Lillemor these days!' she sobbed. 'He didn't say anything at all when she got into his jeep—just as if she owned it!'

Gerard looked uncomfortable.

'Well, I suppose she is his cousin,' he said without much conviction.

'What has that to do with anything?' Elinor demanded. She sniffed and began to look for her non-existent handkerchief. 'He could have said *something*!'

To complete her humiliation, she saw that Gerard was laughing.

'I don't see what's so funny about that!' she said haughtily.

Gerard grinned. 'You wouldn't!' he agreed. 'Poor Elinor! And to think I thought it was all over between you two! In fact I thought it had never really begun! Your father's wishful thinking is really catching, isn't it?'

Elinor coloured and, finding a handkerchief in her bag, blew her nose defiantly.

'I wish it was over!' she snorted defiantly. 'I *hate* him! And her!' she added with determination.

Gerard sighed gently. 'I must say,' he said, 'I wouldn't mind if you hated me like that! I never really had a chance, did I?'

Elinor shook her head. She wished that there was some easy way of saying what she had to, but there was none.

'I'm terribly sorry, Gerard,' she said slowly. 'But even if I wasn't in love with Zachary, it wouldn't have worked out.

One can't get married, or anything, just because one's father would like it that way!'

Gerard patted her hand with his.

'I suppose not,' he agreed regretfully. 'But it might have been nice to have tried all the same. It won't be easy,' he added soberly, 'to tell your father, will it?'

Elinor sniffed again. Somehow she just couldn't stop the tears from pouring down her face.

'There isn't anything to tell him,' she said when she could. 'Nothing has changed, has it? I still don't know what Zachary wants. He's probably making plans right now with Lillemor!'

Gerard frowned, not at all sure how to comfort her.

'I should think that's most unlikely!' he answered. 'I heard him talking about Lillemor going on to England for a visit some time yesterday.'

Elinor stared at him.

'Are you sure?' she demanded.

'Yes, I think so,' he said. He was pleased to see that Elinor's tears had magically dried up. With a sigh of relief he turned his attention back to the road and the miles they had yet to cover. He was more relieved still to see that within a few minutes Elinor had fallen fast asleep.

Although she had only spent two nights out in the open, Elinor was astonished to discover the comfort of her bed at home. Her father, not wishing to admit that he had missed them all, had greeted her with no more than a gruff remark and a rough kiss on her cheek.

'Did you enjoy yourself?' he had asked.

Elinor had nodded happily.

'It was fun!' she had announced. 'I loved every minute of it!'

'Good, good,' he had said vaguely. 'Forgive me, my dear, but I want to talk business with Gerard and see the skins he has brought. You look tired out, why don't you go straight

175

off to your bed.'

'All right, Father,' Elinor had agreed. She had looked round for Lillemor, but there was no sign of the Australian girl. It seemed that she was still with Zachary and it would have been pointless to have stayed up on the offchance that she would be home for dinner. So Elinor had gone up to her room and had allowed the maid to undress her and to draw her bath, revelling in the luxury of being clean after the lack of water in the desert.

She had been in bed some time when her father had come up to see her, carrying her tray with his own hands and grunting slightly from the exertion.

'Most successful!' he said from the doorway. 'Gerard is to be congratulated! Never seen better skins for the price!'

Elinor smiled. 'I think he rather enjoyed himself,' she said. 'It all went off very well!'

Her father peered down at her.

'Humph!' he said. 'Gerard told me some long story. Didn't believe a word of it, of course. Gather that young Zachary of yours came back considerably richer than when he went?'

Elinor blushed. 'I suppose he did,' she said. Her eyes crinkled at the corners with sudden amusement. 'I must say it was a great relief all round when he accepted the Caid's compensation!'

Her father grunted thoughtfully.

'Then he really was held a prisoner for those two years,' he muttered. 'Why didn't he escape?'

'He did!' Elinor retorted, not without pride. 'Twice. As soon as the Tuareg came near enough in he ran away. But the first time he was caught and they beat him, thinking that that would change his mind about leaving them. But he only ran away again. It was walking in the desert that made him so thin!'

Mr. Kendon sat heavily on the edge of her bed.

'It would still be possible for you to be free if you wanted

176

to be,' he said. 'I could arrange it, my dear.'

Elinor lay flat against the pillows preparing herself for the battle that was to come.

'I don't want to be free,' she said.

Her father's face reddened. 'Gerard says he's no longer interested,' he said sharply. 'I can't say I think you played your cards very well as far as he was concerned!'

'No,' she agreed.

Mr. Kendon pushed the tray on to her knees and lifted the covers from the plates.

'You'd better eat something,' he said gruffly. He sat in silence and watched her for a few minutes. 'If it had been anyone but Zachary I could have understood!' he burst out suddenly. 'But why him?'

Elinor shook her head.

'I don't know,' she said. 'It will always be him. But you needn't look so upset, Father. I'm not at all sure that he wants me!'

It hurt that her father should look so relieved.

'You mean he may be after that cousin of his?' he asked hopefully.

But Elinor refused to answer.

'You know, Father,' she said suddenly, 'I don't think that either of us have behaved very well. When Zachary first came back I should have gone to him then, asking no questions. I am his *wife* and I think we both forgot that!'

'And so what are you going to do?' her father asked. His mouth looked pinched and grey and she was worried about him, but even so she knew she couldn't change her mind. She was her father's daughter, but so was she Zachary's wife.

'I'm going to go and live in his house,' she said gently. 'Tomorrow when I go to surgery, I shan't come back here. If he doesn't want me, he'll have to ask me to leave, but meanwhile my place is at his side.'

Mr. Kendon nodded, knowing that he was defeated.

177

'Very well, Elinor,' he said at last. 'I think you're making a mistake, but I won't do anything to stop you.' He stood up and kissed her softly on the brow. 'Good luck, my dear!' he said.

Elinor was a little less sure that she had made the right decision when she walked through the Medina of Meknes the following day on her way to Zachary's surgery. She had packed all her things into a single suitcase and it seemed quite unbearably heavy as she walked along. There was a small stall selling those circular strips of dough that, fried in very hot oil, are so popular with the Moors, and she stopped beside it, buying herself a doughnut so that she could stand and eat it, allowing her hand to recover from the stitching on the handle of her suitcase.

'*Madame.* I shall find you someone to carry that for you!' the stallholder protested. 'It is far too heavy for one as fair as yourself!'

Elinor thanked him, relieved not to have the burden the whole way to Zachary's house. She ate her doughnut slowly and with enjoyment, then set off again with the youth that the stallholder had pressganged into carrying her suitcase coming along a pace or two behind.

Zachary's door stood open. Elinor hesitated for a moment, wondering if she should go first to the surgery, but she had a minute or two yet, so she motioned to the youth to put her suitcase inside the door, tipped him, and then went inside herself.

The sheer beauty of the house struck her anew. It was everything that she had ever dreamed about as a home and as a place in which to bring up children. The latter thought made her blush. She was taking a great deal for granted, she thought grimly, especially as Zachary didn't even know she was coming.

For a long time she stood in the small central garden, noticing that the orange blossom had begun to wither and that the first fruits were beginning to swell among the branches of the tree. They would never be the sweet ones that were so delicious, these were almost wild and the oranges were small and correspondingly bitter, rather like the marmalade variety from Seville. Long ago it had been found better to plant these bitter-bearing trees in public places to deter the passer-by from reaching up into the branches for his breakfast!

So intent was she that she didn't notice Zachary's silent approach. He was dressed in the robes of an Arab and his sandals made no noise at all as he crossed the paved floor.

'The queue has doubled in our absence,' he told her cheerfully. 'I think everyone has heard about our adventures and come to see for themselves!'

Elinor laughed. It seemed a very likely solution.

'Never mind,' she said. 'We have lots of time.'

He looked at her curiously, but he said nothing. Instead he stretched, looking upwards into the sky and blinked at the sun.

'I suppose we'd better get started!' he murmured.

Elinor led the way rather self-consciously to the surgery. She was very much aware of her suitcase sitting in the corner of the garden and she couldn't help hoping in a rather guilty way that Zachary hadn't seen it. It was not going to be easy to explain what she had in mind and, in fact, she was beginning to doubt that she would ever find the courage to do so.

The surgery was filled to overflowing. A dozen women sat behind the screens, most of them with their children leaning against their knees, and all of them laughing and talking at the same time. The men were quieter. They sat and smoked and some of them coughed the dry, hoarse cough that smoking hashish gives, because so many of them smoked it where in the West a man would drink his pint at the local pub.

Elinor took one look at the hubbub which surrounded her

and began to try to restore some sort of order. The patients were amenable enough. They had come to see Si Zachary and as soon as he entered a hush fell over them and they sat quite still, staring at him with their soft, liquid eyes, wondering at the stories that had already travelled throughout the *souks* the length and breadth of Morocco.

Elinor sorted them vaguely into groups, trying to deal with the children first so that they and their mothers could go home. But nobody went. As soon as they had seen the doctor, they sat themselves down again and went on talking as happily as before.

'You'll have to clear them out group by group,' Zachary suggested.

Elinor looked at the rapidly increasing numbers and sighed.

'I think the best thing would be to have two surgeries,' she said at last. 'One for the women and children and one for the men.'

Zachary bent over his instruments.

'Yes? Could you manage to come along twice a day?'

Elinor thought of her suitcase and blushed. She muttered something which turned out to be nothing in particular and fled back into the waiting room. She couldn't go through with it, she thought. When the surgery came to an end, she would just pick up her suitcase and walk home the way she had come!

With remarkable energy, she said farewell to at least six of the women and pushed them out of the door into the street. The children clutched the sweets that Zachary had given them and pulled at their mothers' skirts to attract attention to their prizes. The noise was quite unbelievable and yet slowly, almost incredibly, the numbers began to go down and there were only a few men waiting patiently for their turn.

When at last Zachary had seen the last one, he came into the waiting room to wash his hands for the last time.

'Do you think you could go through and see if Lillemor has got here yet?' he asked Elinor.

To her it seemed as if in that one sentence all her dreams had crumbled into dust. She got up stiffly, feeling the full weight of the heat and the continuous press of people she had suffered for the last couple of hours.

'Is she coming here again tonight?' she couldn't resist asking.

Zachary watched her closely.

'She's looking in,' he said.

Elinor didn't dare look at him again. She shut the waiting room door after her and walked through into the little garden. Her suitcase was still standing where she had left it and she gave it a quick push into a less conspicuous position. It was the last thing that she wanted Lillemor to see.

The Australian girl was sitting by the fountain that played at intervals in one corner of the garden. She looked up when she saw Elinor, but she made no attempt to smile or, indeed, to greet her in any way.

'We've just about finished,' Elinor told her. 'Zachary is just writing out the last prescription.'

Lillemor pouted and dabbled her hand in the water beside her.

'Do you know, when I first saw you,' she said clearly, 'I thought you would be easy to manage, but you're not, are you?'

Elinor looked baffled.

'In what way?' she asked uncomfortably.

Lillemor frowned at her. 'In what way should I mean?' she asked irritably. 'I mean as far as Zachary is concerned! You never seemed to lift a finger and yet you won all the same.'

'Did I?' Elinor said dryly. 'I wish I could be as sure!' She cast a quick look at her suitcase protruding out of a flower-bed and shivered despite the heat.

Lillemor gave her a curious look.

'Oh well,' she said with a faint smile, 'if anything ever happens, perhaps you'll give me first refusal? Of Zachary, I mean!'

Elinor smiled too. She had to admire Lillemor's courage and she liked her more than she had ever done.

'Yes, I will,' she agreed. 'But wouldn't it be better for you to find someone else?'

'Who?' Lillemor asked reasonably. 'Gerard?'

Elinor nodded. 'He's very nice,' she said.

Lillemor made a face.

'Not to me, honey! That boy is completely wrapped up in his skins! But I'll bear the idea in mind. Perhaps one of those swinging Englishmen will be the answer!'

'The answer to what?' Zachary asked from the doorway.

Elinor blushed vividly, but Lillemor remained calm and perfectly cool.

'Never you mind!' she drawled softly. 'Give me my tickets and let me go!'

Zachary handed her over a travel agent's folder, pointing out to her her sailing ticket from Gibraltar and her air-ticket from Tangier across the Straits to the Spanish mainland.

'There's some pocket money in it too,' he told her carefully. 'You can call it a repayment to your father for all he did for me.'

Lillemor peered into the pocket and pulled out an assortment of traveller's cheques for about three hundred pounds.

'Perhaps you value me more than I thought,' she commented. 'What a pity it isn't a little bit more!'

Zachary's face looked very lean and ascetic.

'You'll be happier in England,' he said.

Lillemor stood up and sauntered over to the door that led into the street. There she paused and raised a hand in farewell to them both.

'No doubt!' she said, and disappeared into the street.

They could hear her high heels on the cobbles outside as she walked away from them, and then there was silence and only the shuffle of the Arab sandals coming from the main alley.

Elinor reached up and picked a dead flower off the orange tree. With her face averted from Zachary she thought she could think better, but she was still terribly conscious of him as he stood in silence, standing as easily as a man from the desert, as if the whole of time belonged to him.

'What is Lillemor going to do?' she asked at last, when she could bear the silence no longer.

'She's going to take a look at England. She has friends there,' he answered. 'Perhaps one day she'll come back to Morocco, but it won't be for a long time yet.'

Elinor dropped the dead blossom and ran her hands down her apron.

'It seems funny being home again, doesn't it?' she remarked.

Zachary looked at her closely.

'I suppose,' he said, 'that I ought to be walking you home to your father now?'

Elinor coloured, but she stood her ground.

'I'm not going back tonight,' she said.

His eyebrows shot up, giving him a satanic look. 'You're not?'

She licked her lips, searching for something devastating to say.

'No,' she said pugnaciously.

Zachary drew himself up to his full height. In his Arab robes he looked taller and thinner than ever and she was more than a little afraid of him.

'May one ask why not?' His voice sounded strange and as distant as a far off storm.

'I'm your wife,' Elinor muttered defensively.

'So,' he said, 'you've finally remembered that?'

183

Elinor gave him an angry look. She couldn't think why she wanted to stay with him! He was perfectly horrid when he looked at her like that, just as if it had all been her fault and that he had had nothing to do with it!

'I always did remember it!' she assured him hotly. 'A great deal more often than it was comfortable! But as you had nothing to say, what was I to do?'

Zachary still looked a little like an avenging angel, but there was a softening in the expression on his face that made her heart beat nineteen to the dozen.

'You could have trusted me,' he said.

She held her head very high. 'You could have trusted *me*!' she retorted. 'How was I to know that you wanted me at all?'

Zachary's mouth twitched dangerously.

'I should have thought that I made that pretty clear!' he said.

'Well, you didn't!' she said hotly. 'I—I thought you didn't want me any more. I almost got used to the idea! I thought you wanted Lillemor,' she added unwisely.

Zachary looked astonished.

'But she's my cousin!' he exclaimed.

'What's that got to do with it?' she asked sourly.

He shrugged his shoulders, openly laughing at her.

'I was brought up with her,' he explained patiently. 'She's practically my sister!'

It was on the tip of her tongue to tell him that Lillemor didn't feel like his sister at all, but that, after all, was the Australian girl's secret.

'Well, I wish you'd said so sooner!' she said instead.

Zachary shook his head at her. 'I suppose Garard was a flash in the pan?' he confronted her.

To his surprise, Elinor giggled. 'Not even that!' she told him. 'I like him very much, but that isn't the same thing, is it?'

Zachary's mouth twitched with amusement.

'Not exactly,' he agreed dryly. He held out his hand to her and, when she took it, drew her into the circle of his arms. 'I'm hungry,' he said in the most unromantic tones. 'I'll take your suitcase inside and then we can eat!'

But Elinor was not yet ready to eat.

'Just kiss me once,' she pleaded. 'I want to be sure it will be just the same as last time!'

He grinned at her. 'It won't be,' he warned her. 'We're two different people now. But it will be nicer this time!'

'Will it?' For a minute she was not sure. It had been so lovely when she had first fallen in love with him and when they had been married in her father's *patio*. But now she knew how easily happiness could slip from one's grasp and she was afraid.

'It will be better,' Zachary said against her lips, 'because this time we're not a boy and girl, but man and wife!'

He kissed her gently at first and then, as passion grew between them, he held her tightly against his thin body and kissed her again.

'There!' he said in triumph. 'Could anything be better than that?'

But Elinor didn't answer him. She could not, because he was kissing her again.

The warm smell of burning charcoal filled the little garden. Elinor renewed her efforts to fan it from a maroon colour to a bright scarlet. Zachary lay on a pile of cushions and watched her, smiling at her fierce concentration.

'I suppose I shall have to buy you a proper stove,' he said reluctantly.

'Yes, you will. We'll have to eat something else besides *couscous* sometimes!'

He grinned. 'And you'll want something that will cook all those milk slops for the children!' he teased her.

Elinor's concentration was completely broken for an instant and he whooped joyously at having made her blush.

185

'Or don't you intend to have any?' he asked her.

Elinor fanned at the charcoal.

'Not until I've fattened you up a bit,' she retorted in an admirably calm voice. 'At the moment your bones stick out in the most unexpected places.'

Zachary chuckled appreciatively.

'My love, I delight in your conversation,' he said, 'but I delight in your kisses more. Can't you leave that damned food to cook itself and come over here?'

Elinor replaced the *couscous* pan on to the brazier and came slowly over to where he was sitting.

'Well?' she asked him.

He smiled up at her.

'I want to hear how much you love me,' he said. 'I can still scarcely believe you're with me again.'

She sat down on the cushions beside him and turned into his arms.

'I love you,' she said softly. 'I love you as the desert loves the rain, as the birds singing in the sun. I love you more than any words can say!'

He went white, as if he could hardly believe that he had heard her aright.

'And I,' he said in a funny gruff voice, 'I love you more than any other woman has ever been loved in Morocco, in the land of the farthest west!'

Harlequin Collection Editions

*Please note: The number in brackets indicates the
original Harlequin Romance number.*

Harlequin Collection Editions

Please note: The number in brackets indicates the original Harlequin Romance number.

Harlequin Collection Editions

Please note: The number in brackets indicates the original Harlequin Romance number.

Harlequin Collection Editions

Please note: The number in brackets indicates the original Harlequin Romance number.

Complete and mail this coupon today!